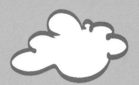

SUPERMAN® FAMILY ADVENTURES™

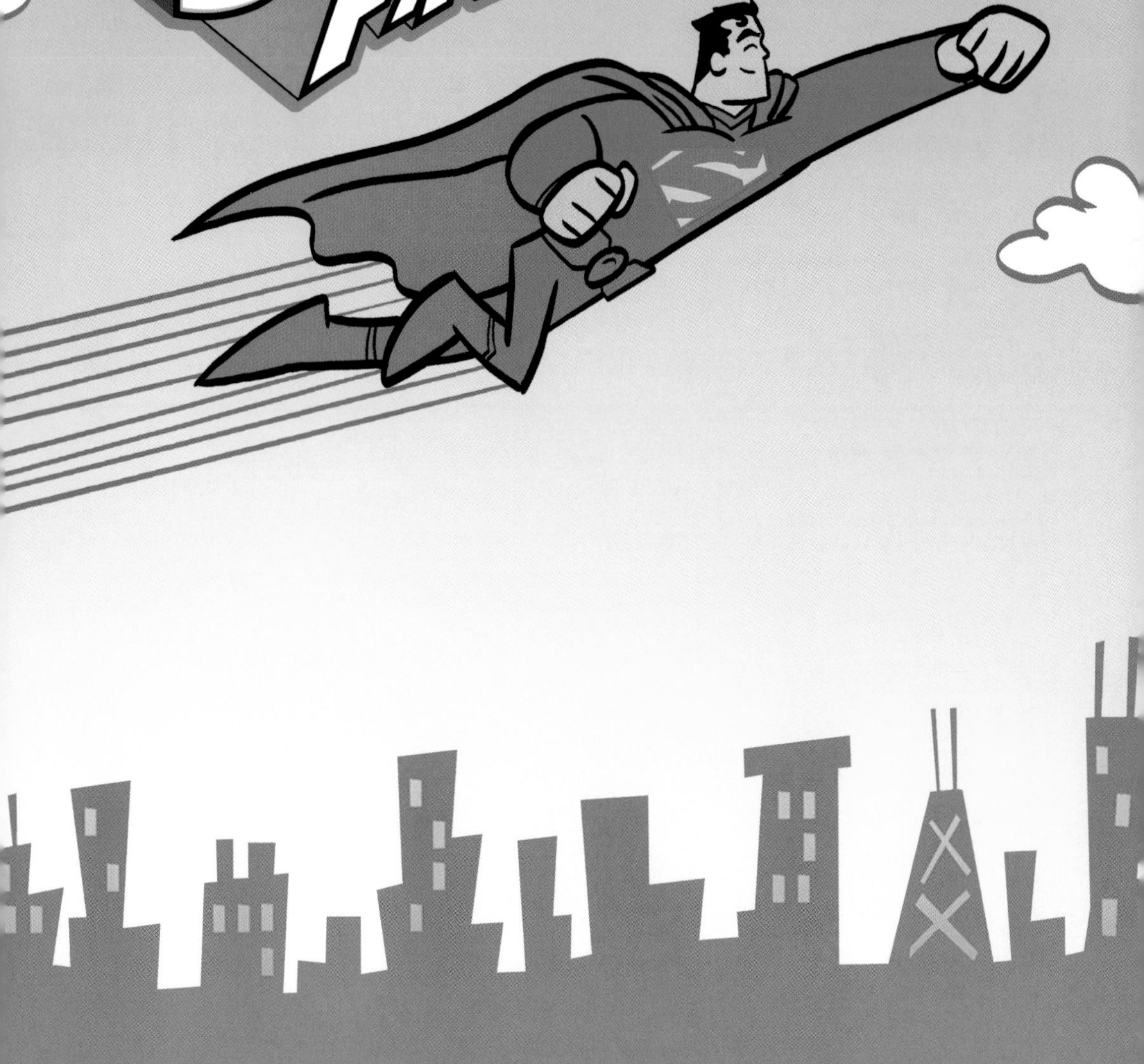

STONE ARCH BOOKS
a capstone imprint

 STONE ARCH BOOKS®

Published in 2014
A Capstone Imprint
1710 Roe Crest Drive
North Mankato, MN 56003
www.capstonepub.com

Originally published by DC Comics in the U.S. in single
magazine form as SUPERMAN FAMILY ADVENTURES #11.
Copyright © 2014 DC Comics. All Rights Reserved.

DC Comics
1700 Broadway, New York, NY 10019
A Warner Bros. Entertainment Company

Cataloging-in-Publication Data is available at the
Library of Congress website:
ISBN: 978-1-4342-9006-9 (library binding)

Summary: MA KENT finally meets LOIS LANE! What startling questions
might they have for one another?

STONE ARCH BOOKS
Ashley C. Andersen Zantop Publisher
Michael Dahl Editorial Director
Donald Lemke & Sean Tulien Editors
Brann Garvey & Russell Griesmer Designers
Kathy McColley Production Specialist

DC COMICS
Kristy Quinn Original U.S. Editor

Printed in China by Nordica.
1013/CA21301918
092013 007744NORDS14

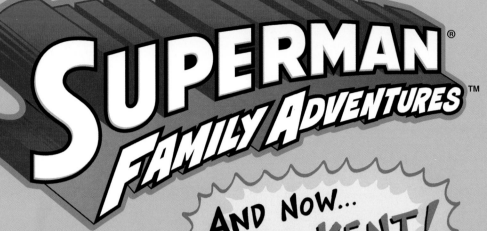

SUPERMAN® FAMILY ADVENTURES™

AND NOW... MA KENT!

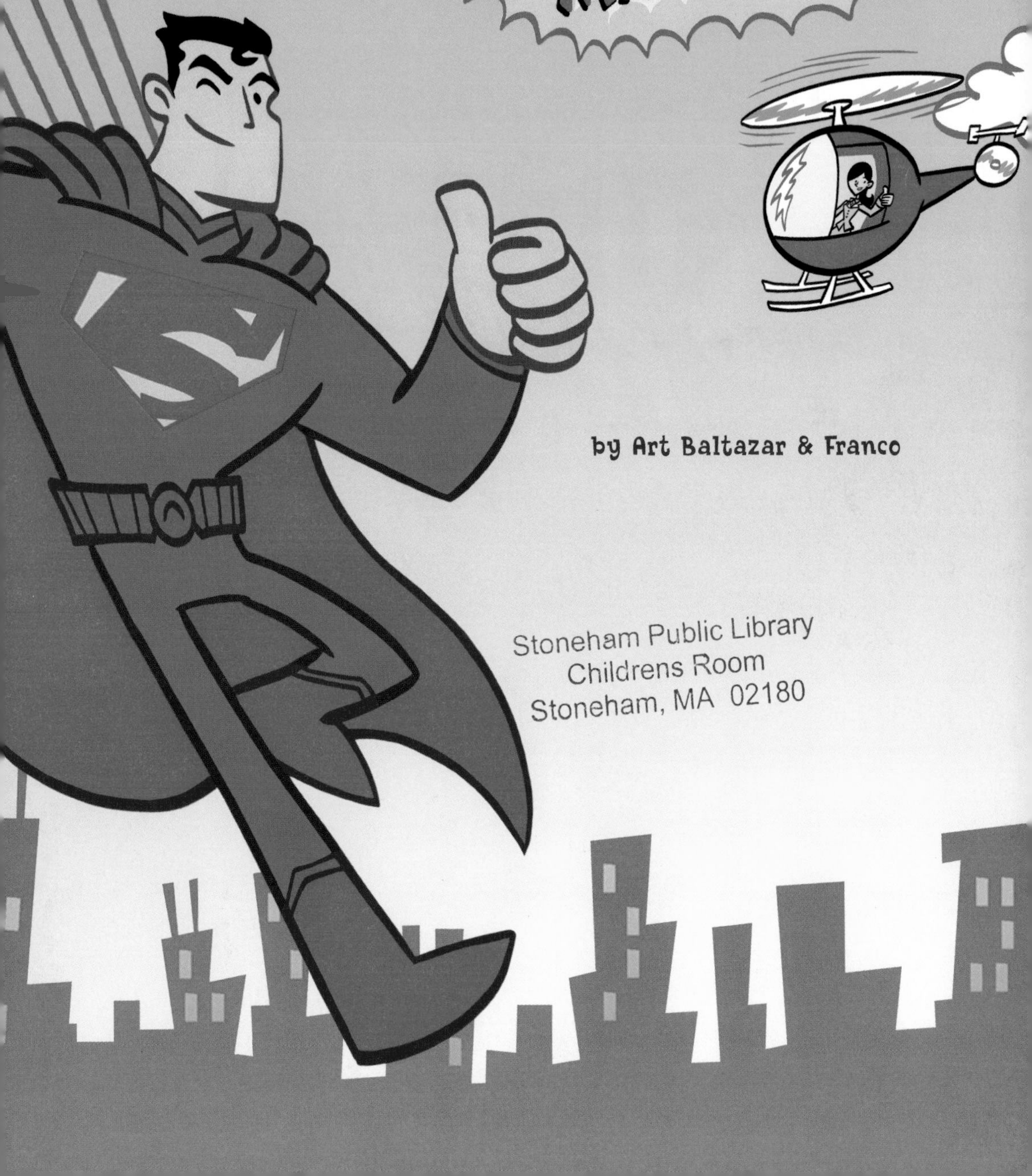

by Art Baltazar & Franco

SUPERMAN® FAMILY ADVENTURES™

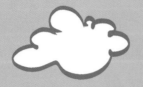

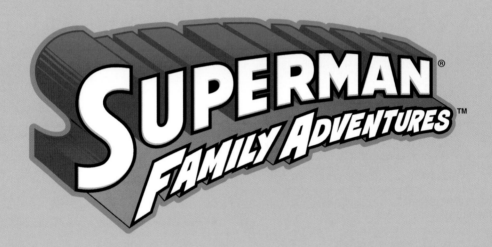

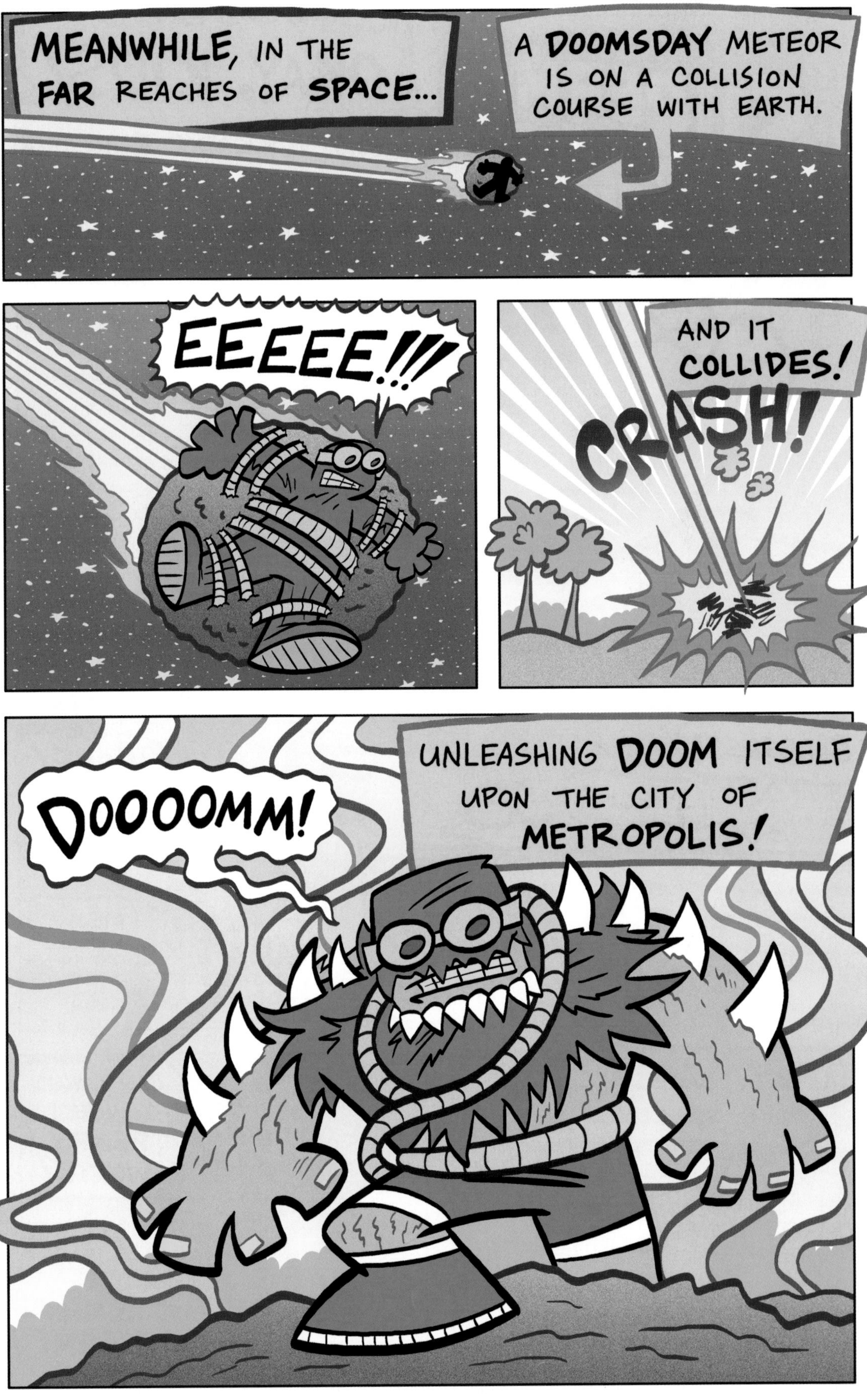
MEANWHILE, IN THE FAR REACHES OF SPACE...
A DOOMSDAY METEOR IS ON A COLLISION COURSE WITH EARTH.
EEEEE!!!
AND IT COLLIDES!
CRASH!
DOOOOMM!
UNLEASHING DOOM ITSELF UPON THE CITY OF METROPOLIS!

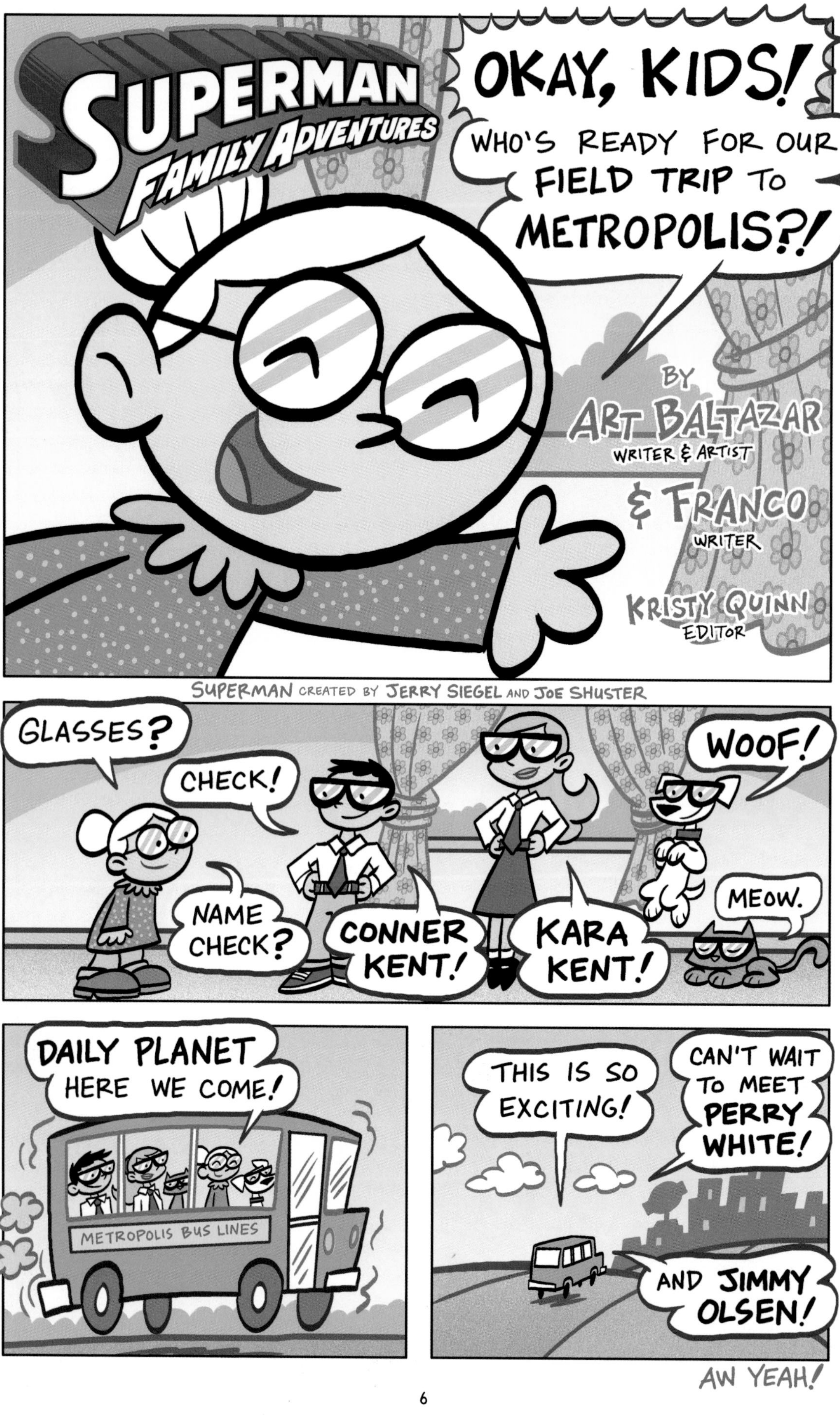
SUPERMAN FAMILY ADVENTURES
OKAY, KIDS!
WHO'S READY FOR OUR FIELD TRIP TO METROPOLIS?!
BY ART BALTAZAR WRITER & ARTIST
& FRANCO WRITER
KRISTY QUINN EDITOR
SUPERMAN CREATED BY JERRY SIEGEL AND JOE SHUSTER
GLASSES?
CHECK!
WOOF!
NAME CHECK?
CONNER KENT!
KARA KENT!
MEOW.
DAILY PLANET HERE WE COME!
METROPOLIS BUS LINES
THIS IS SO EXCITING!
CAN'T WAIT TO MEET PERRY WHITE!
AND JIMMY OLSEN!
AW YEAH!

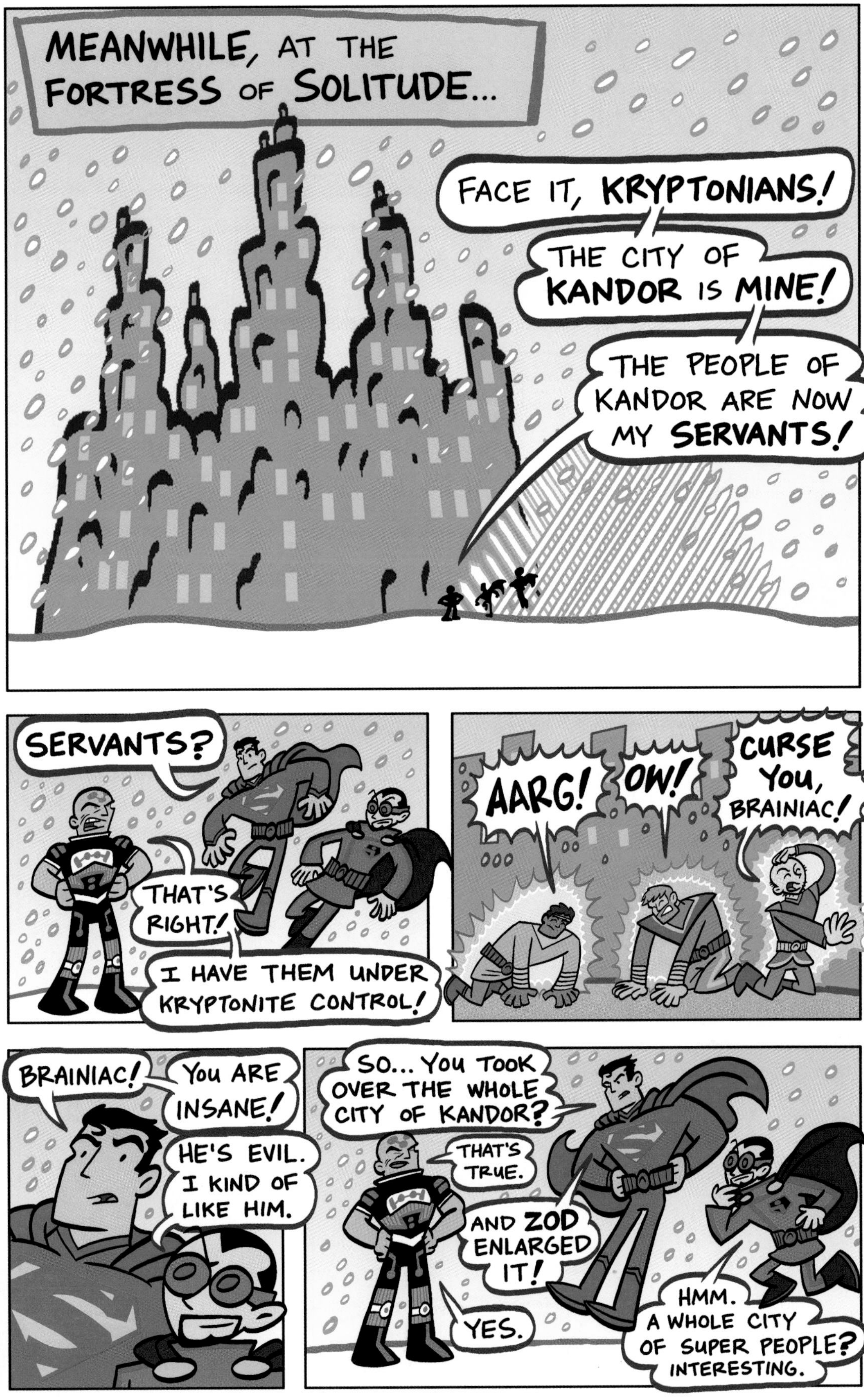
MEANWHILE, AT THE FORTRESS OF SOLITUDE...
FACE IT, KRYPTONIANS!
THE CITY OF KANDOR IS MINE!
THE PEOPLE OF KANDOR ARE NOW MY SERVANTS!
SERVANTS?
THAT'S RIGHT!
I HAVE THEM UNDER KRYPTONITE CONTROL!
AARG!
OW!
CURSE YOU, BRAINIAC!
BRAINIAC!
YOU ARE INSANE!
HE'S EVIL. I KIND OF LIKE HIM.
SO... YOU TOOK OVER THE WHOLE CITY OF KANDOR?
THAT'S TRUE.
AND ZOD ENLARGED IT!
YES.
HMM. A WHOLE CITY OF SUPER PEOPLE? INTERESTING.

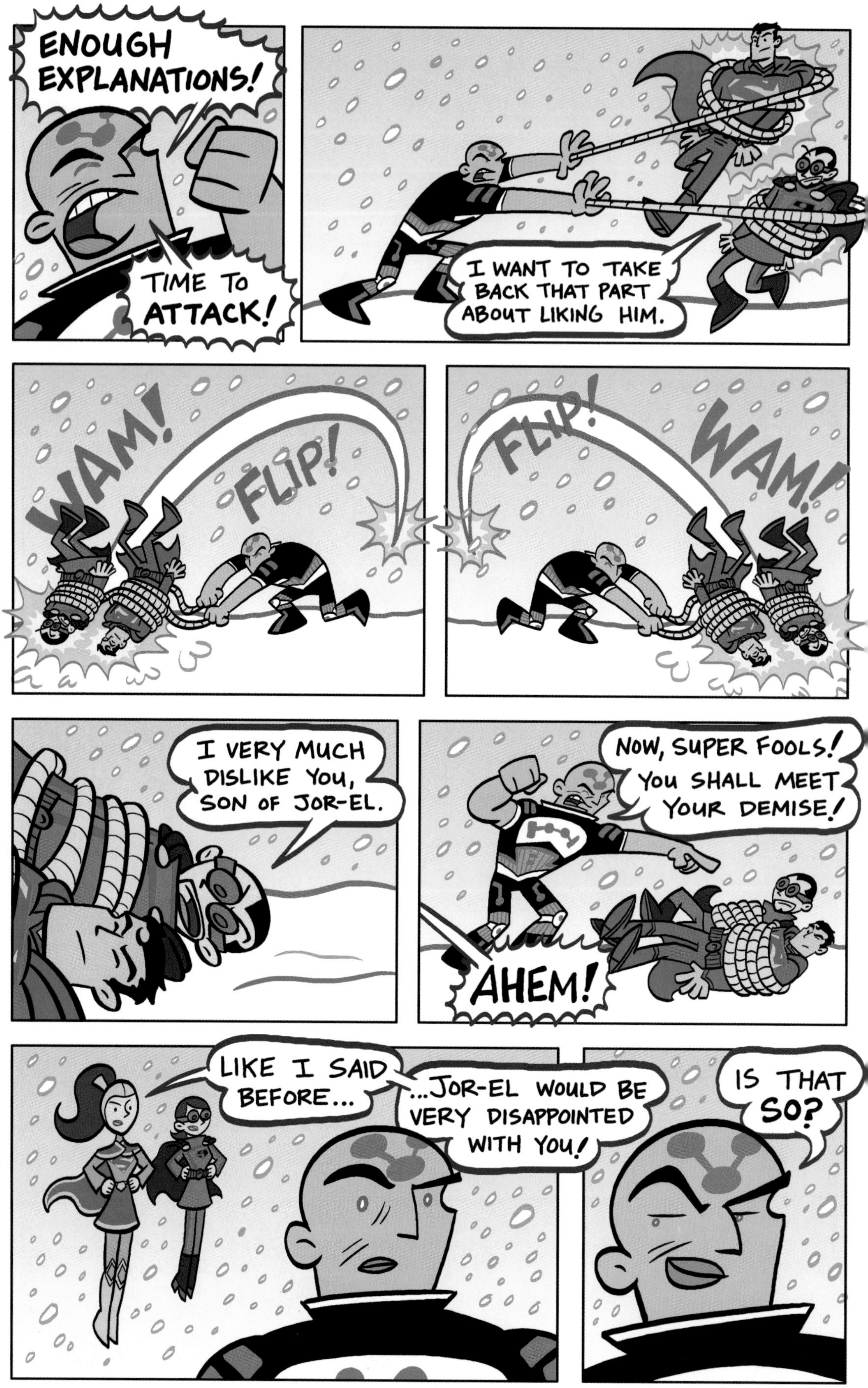

ENOUGH EXPLANATIONS!
TIME TO ATTACK!
I WANT TO TAKE BACK THAT PART ABOUT LIKING HIM.
WAM!
FLIP!
FLIP!
WAM!
I VERY MUCH DISLIKE YOU, SON OF JOR-EL.
NOW, SUPER FOOLS! YOU SHALL MEET YOUR DEMISE!
AHEM!
LIKE I SAID BEFORE...
...JOR-EL WOULD BE VERY DISAPPOINTED WITH YOU!
IS THAT SO?

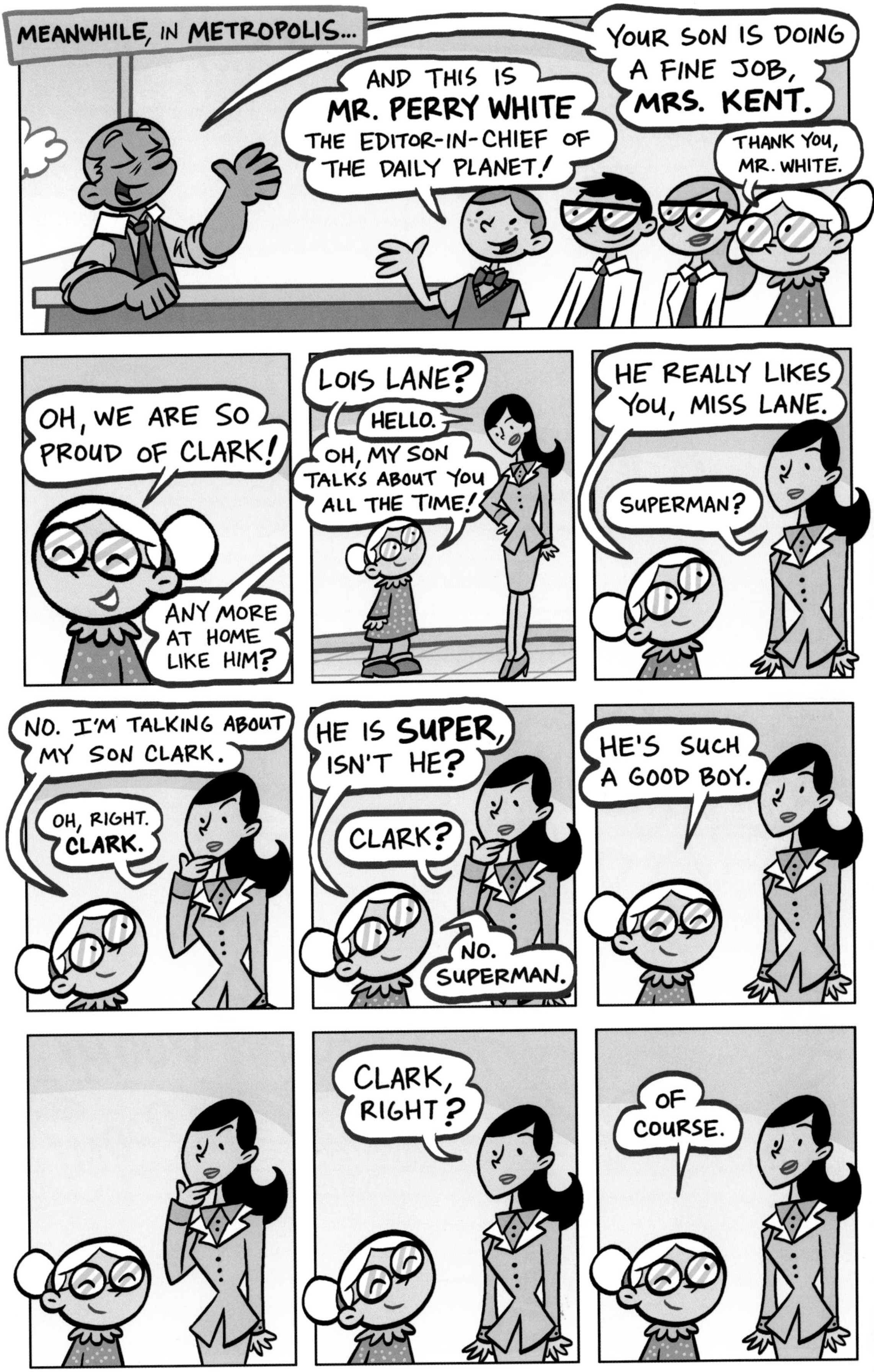
MEANWHILE, IN METROPOLIS...
AND THIS IS MR. PERRY WHITE THE EDITOR-IN-CHIEF OF THE DAILY PLANET!
YOUR SON IS DOING A FINE JOB, MRS. KENT.
THANK YOU, MR. WHITE.
OH, WE ARE SO PROUD OF CLARK!
ANY MORE AT HOME LIKE HIM?
LOIS LANE?
HELLO.
OH, MY SON TALKS ABOUT YOU ALL THE TIME!
HE REALLY LIKES YOU, MISS LANE.
SUPERMAN?
NO. I'M TALKING ABOUT MY SON CLARK.
OH, RIGHT. CLARK.
HE IS SUPER, ISN'T HE?
CLARK?
NO. SUPERMAN.
HE'S SUCH A GOOD BOY.
CLARK, RIGHT?
OF COURSE.

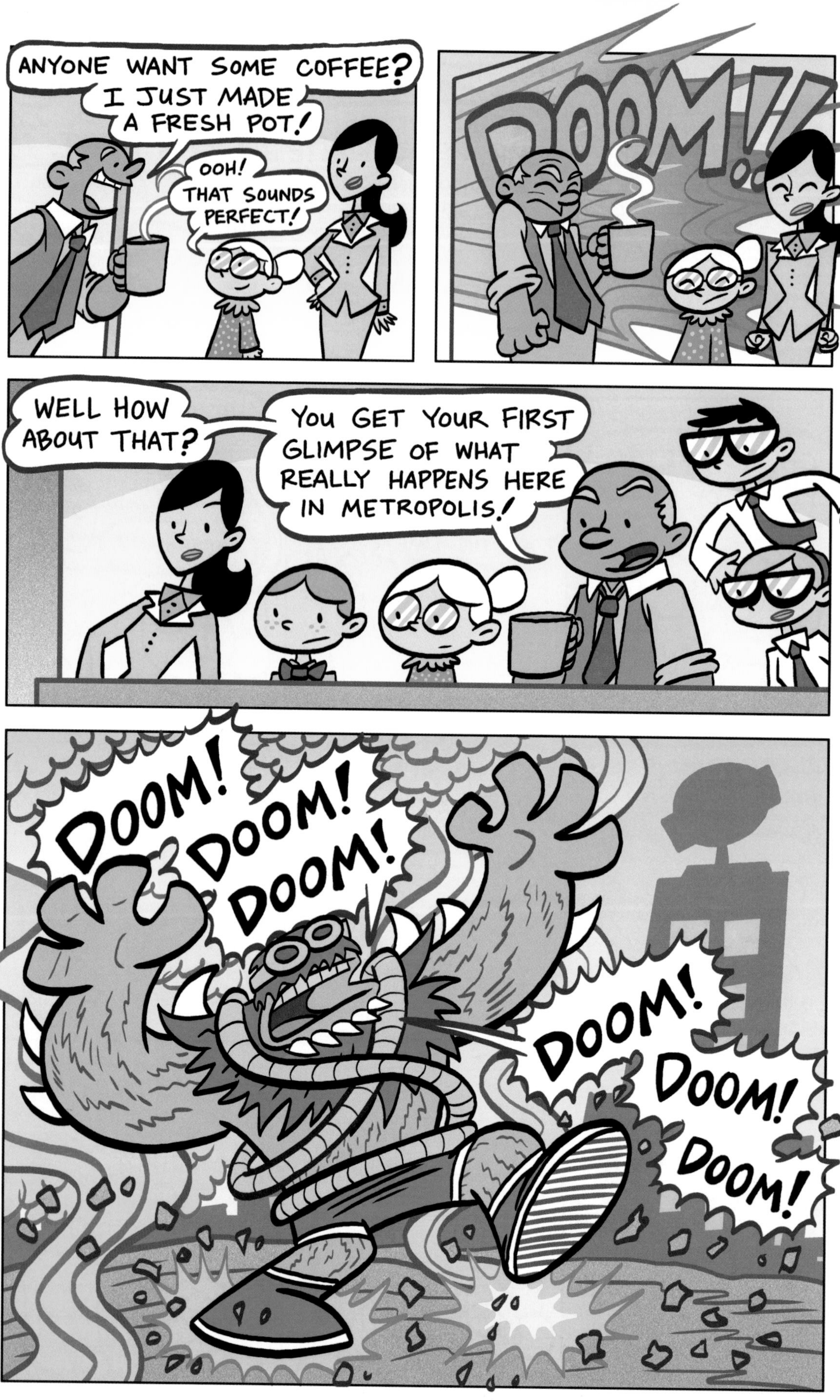
ANYONE WANT SOME COFFEE? I JUST MADE A FRESH POT!
OOH! THAT SOUNDS PERFECT!
DOOM!!
WELL HOW ABOUT THAT?
YOU GET YOUR FIRST GLIMPSE OF WHAT REALLY HAPPENS HERE IN METROPOLIS!
DOOM! DOOM! DOOM!
DOOM! DOOM! DOOM!

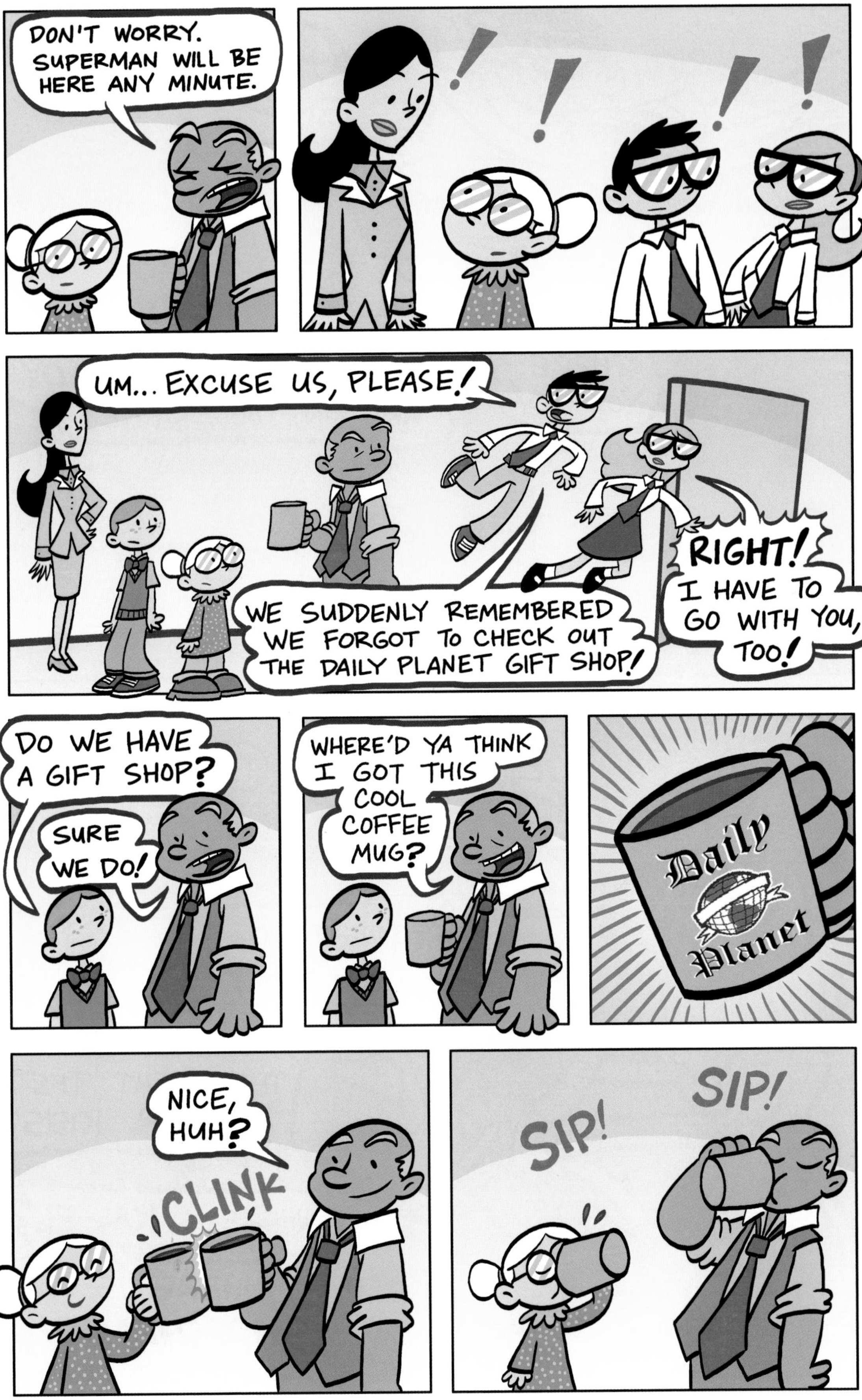
DON'T WORRY. SUPERMAN WILL BE HERE ANY MINUTE.
UM... EXCUSE US, PLEASE!
WE SUDDENLY REMEMBERED WE FORGOT TO CHECK OUT THE DAILY PLANET GIFT SHOP!
RIGHT! I HAVE TO GO WITH YOU, TOO!
DO WE HAVE A GIFT SHOP?
SURE WE DO!
WHERE'D YA THINK I GOT THIS COOL COFFEE MUG?
Daily Planet
NICE, HUH?
CLINK
SIP!
SIP!

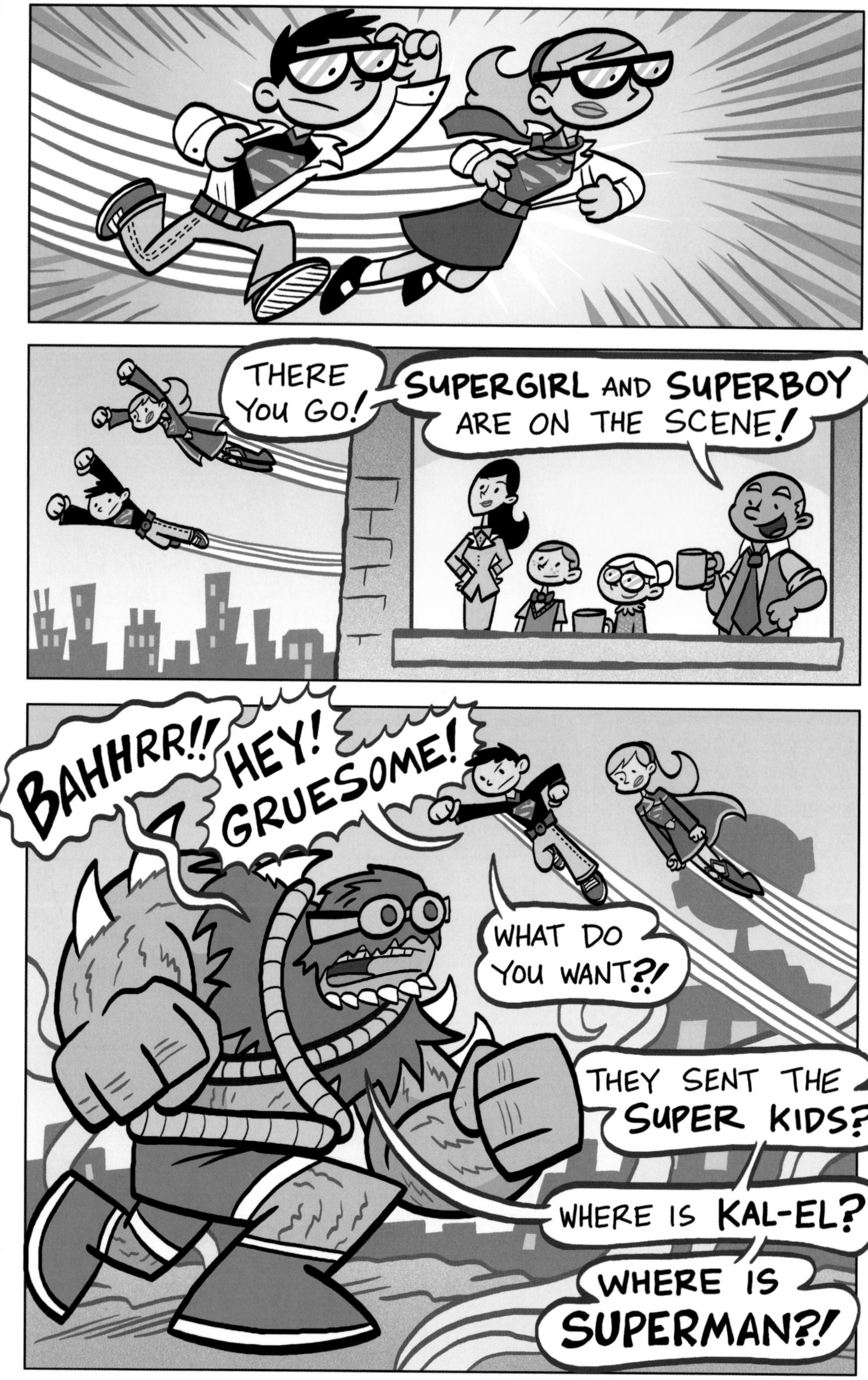
THERE YOU GO!
SUPERGIRL AND SUPERBOY ARE ON THE SCENE!
BAHHRR!!
HEY! GRUESOME!
WHAT DO YOU WANT?!
THEY SENT THE SUPER KIDS?
WHERE IS KAL-EL?
WHERE IS SUPERMAN?!

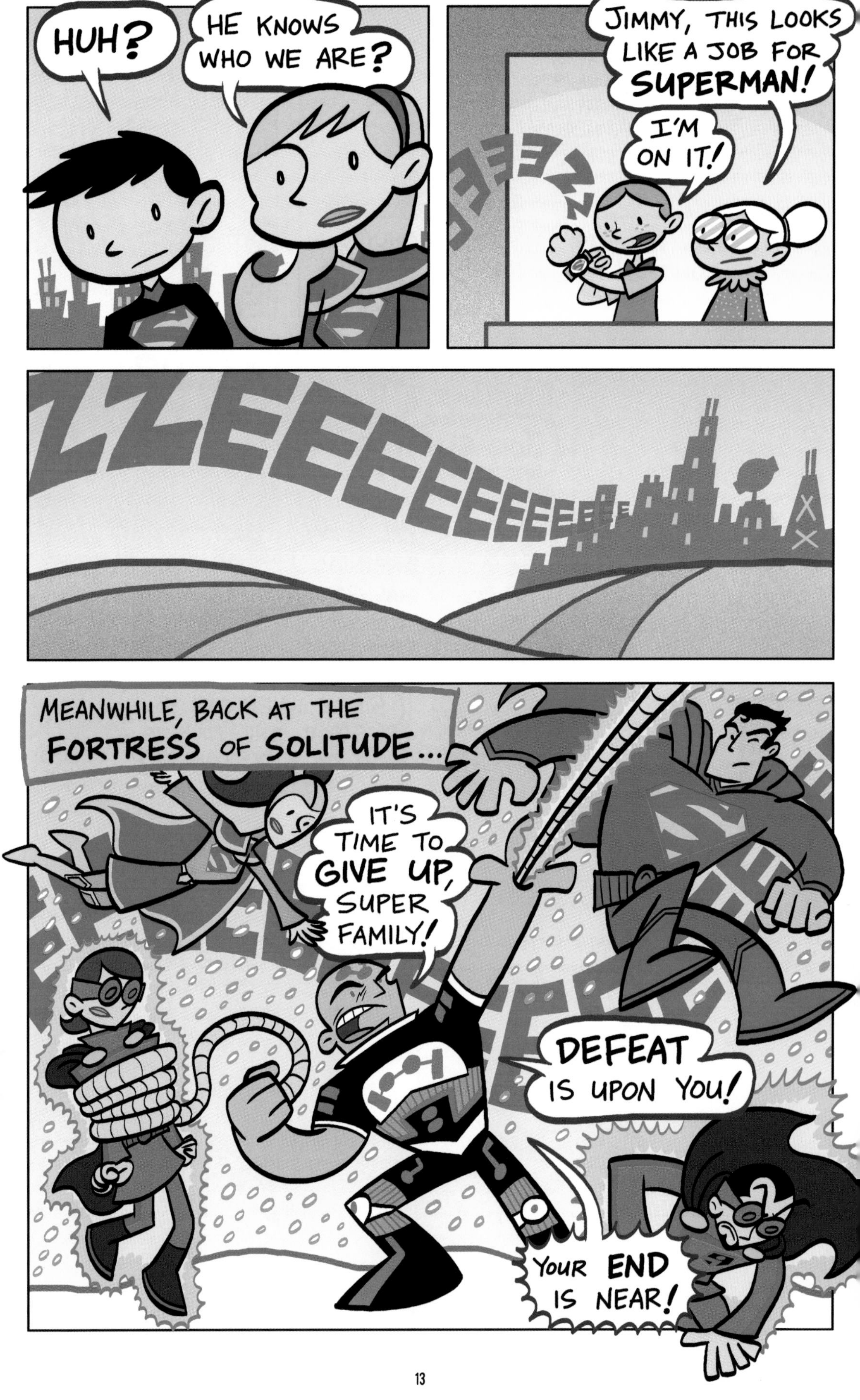
HUH?
HE KNOWS WHO WE ARE?
JIMMY, THIS LOOKS LIKE A JOB FOR SUPERMAN!
I'M ON IT!
ZZEEEEEEEEEEEEE
MEANWHILE, BACK AT THE FORTRESS OF SOLITUDE...
IT'S TIME TO GIVE UP, SUPER FAMILY!
DEFEAT IS UPON YOU!
YOUR END IS NEAR!

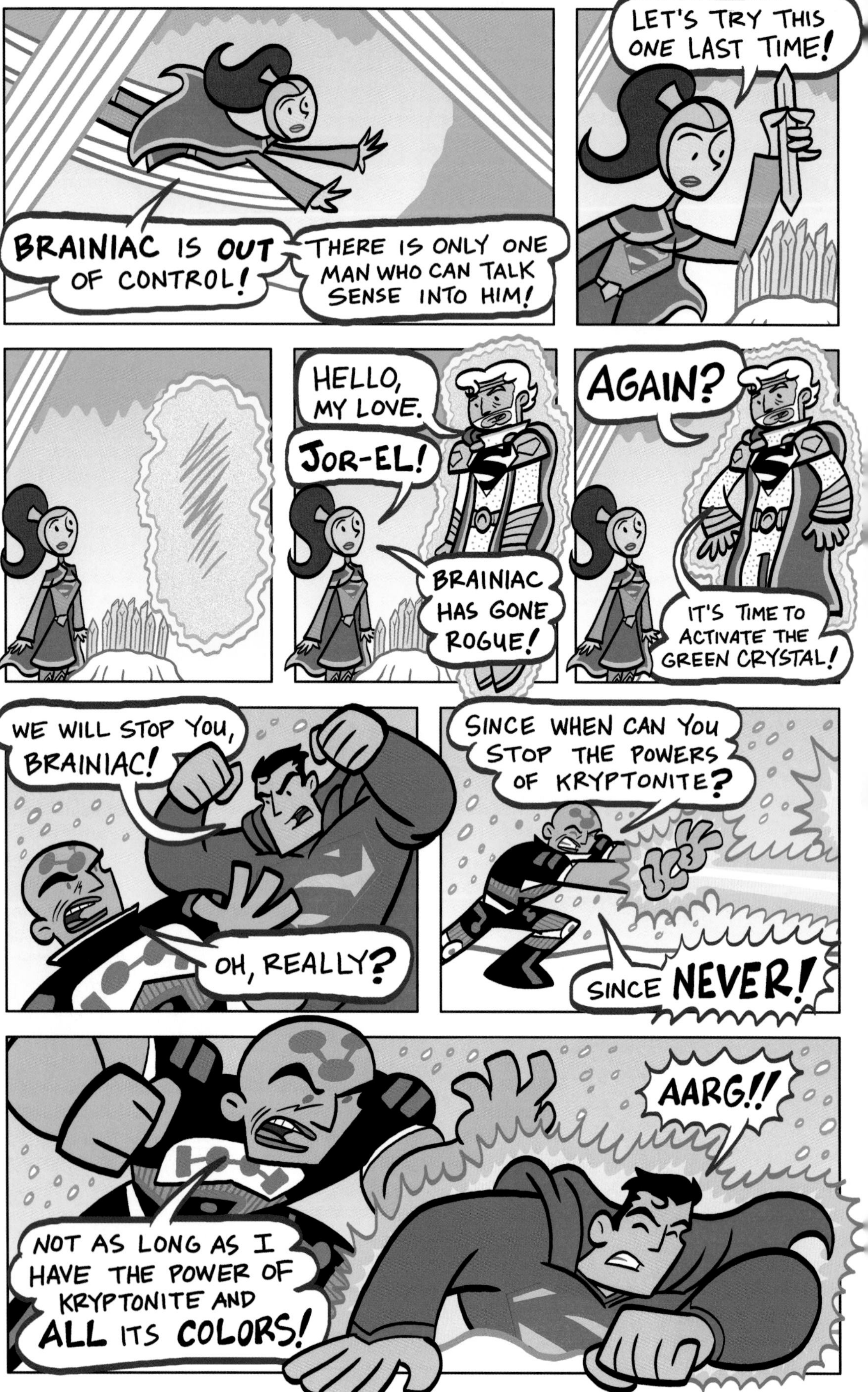
BRAINIAC IS OUT OF CONTROL!
THERE IS ONLY ONE MAN WHO CAN TALK SENSE INTO HIM!
LET'S TRY THIS ONE LAST TIME!
HELLO, MY LOVE.
JOR-EL!
BRAINIAC HAS GONE ROGUE!
AGAIN?
IT'S TIME TO ACTIVATE THE GREEN CRYSTAL!
WE WILL STOP YOU, BRAINIAC!
OH, REALLY?
SINCE WHEN CAN YOU STOP THE POWERS OF KRYPTONITE?
SINCE NEVER!
AARG!!
NOT AS LONG AS I HAVE THE POWER OF KRYPTONITE AND ALL ITS COLORS!

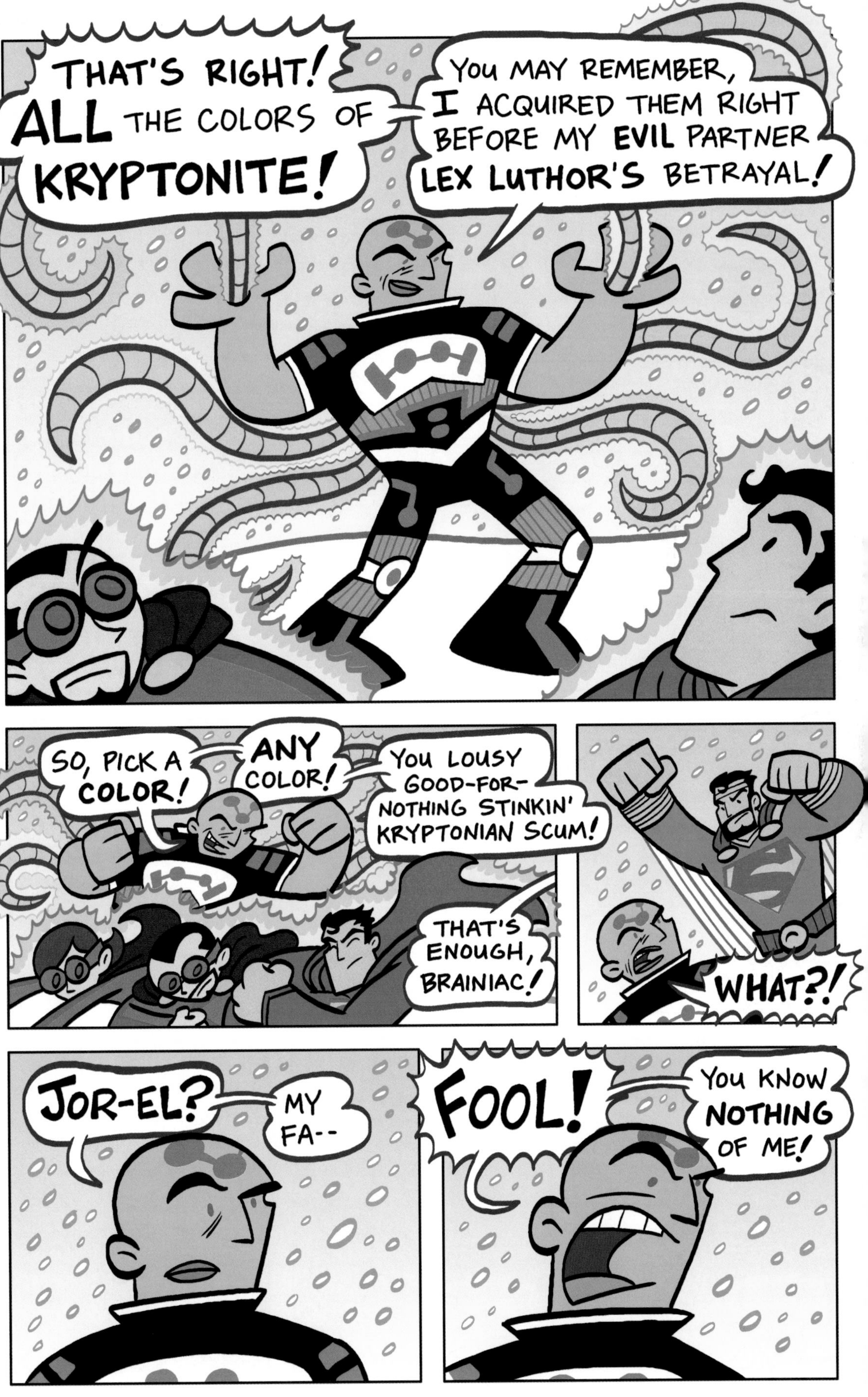
THAT'S RIGHT! ALL THE COLORS OF KRYPTONITE!
YOU MAY REMEMBER, I ACQUIRED THEM RIGHT BEFORE MY EVIL PARTNER LEX LUTHOR'S BETRAYAL!
SO, PICK A COLOR!
ANY COLOR!
YOU LOUSY GOOD-FOR-NOTHING STINKIN' KRYPTONIAN SCUM!
THAT'S ENOUGH, BRAINIAC!
WHAT?!
JOR-EL?
MY FA--
FOOL!
YOU KNOW NOTHING OF ME!

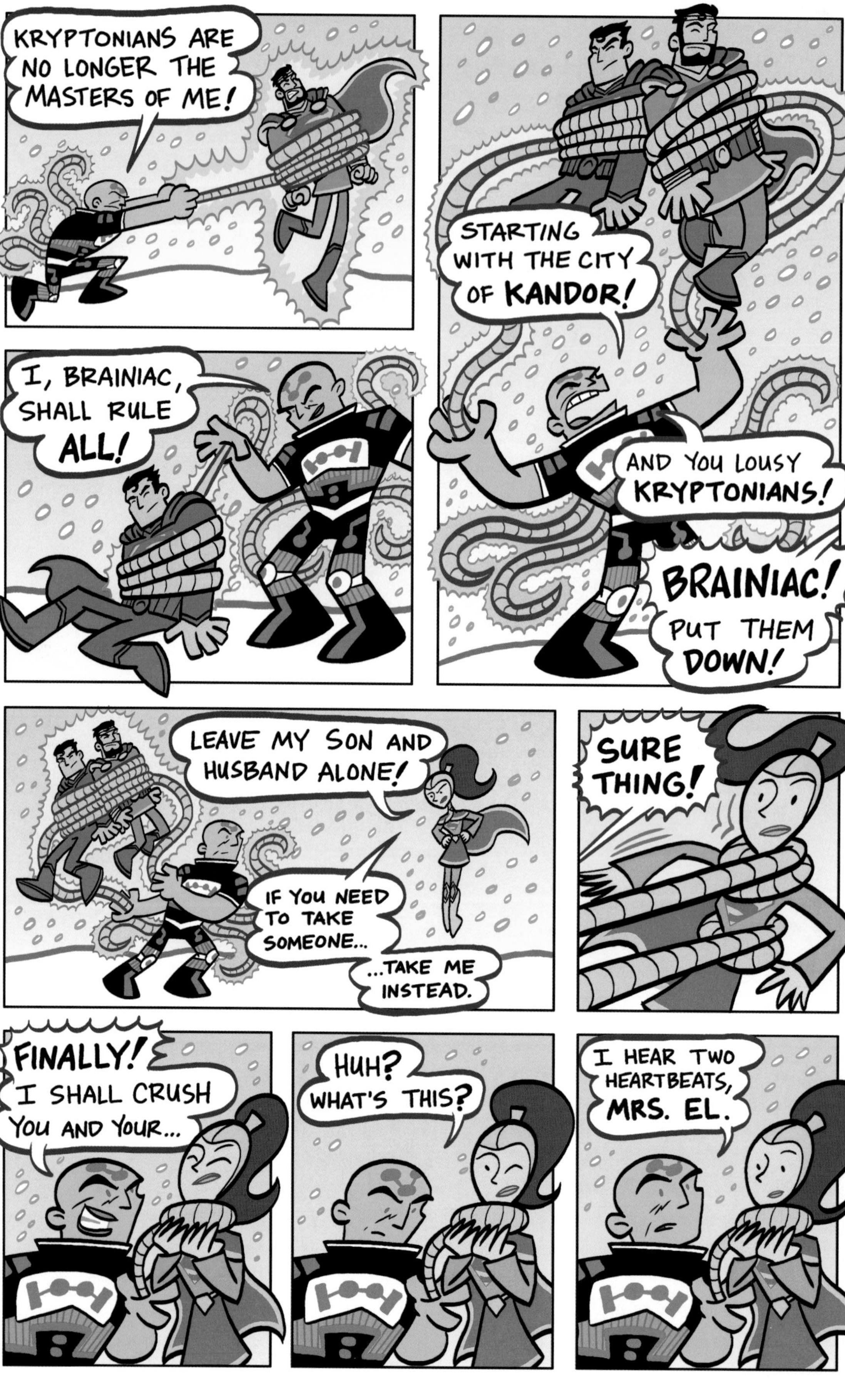

KRYPTONIANS ARE NO LONGER THE MASTERS OF ME!
STARTING WITH THE CITY OF KANDOR!
I, BRAINIAC, SHALL RULE ALL!
AND YOU LOUSY KRYPTONIANS!
BRAINIAC! PUT THEM DOWN!
LEAVE MY SON AND HUSBAND ALONE!
IF YOU NEED TO TAKE SOMEONE...
...TAKE ME INSTEAD.
SURE THING!
FINALLY! I SHALL CRUSH YOU AND YOUR...
HUH? WHAT'S THIS?
I HEAR TWO HEARTBEATS, MRS. EL.

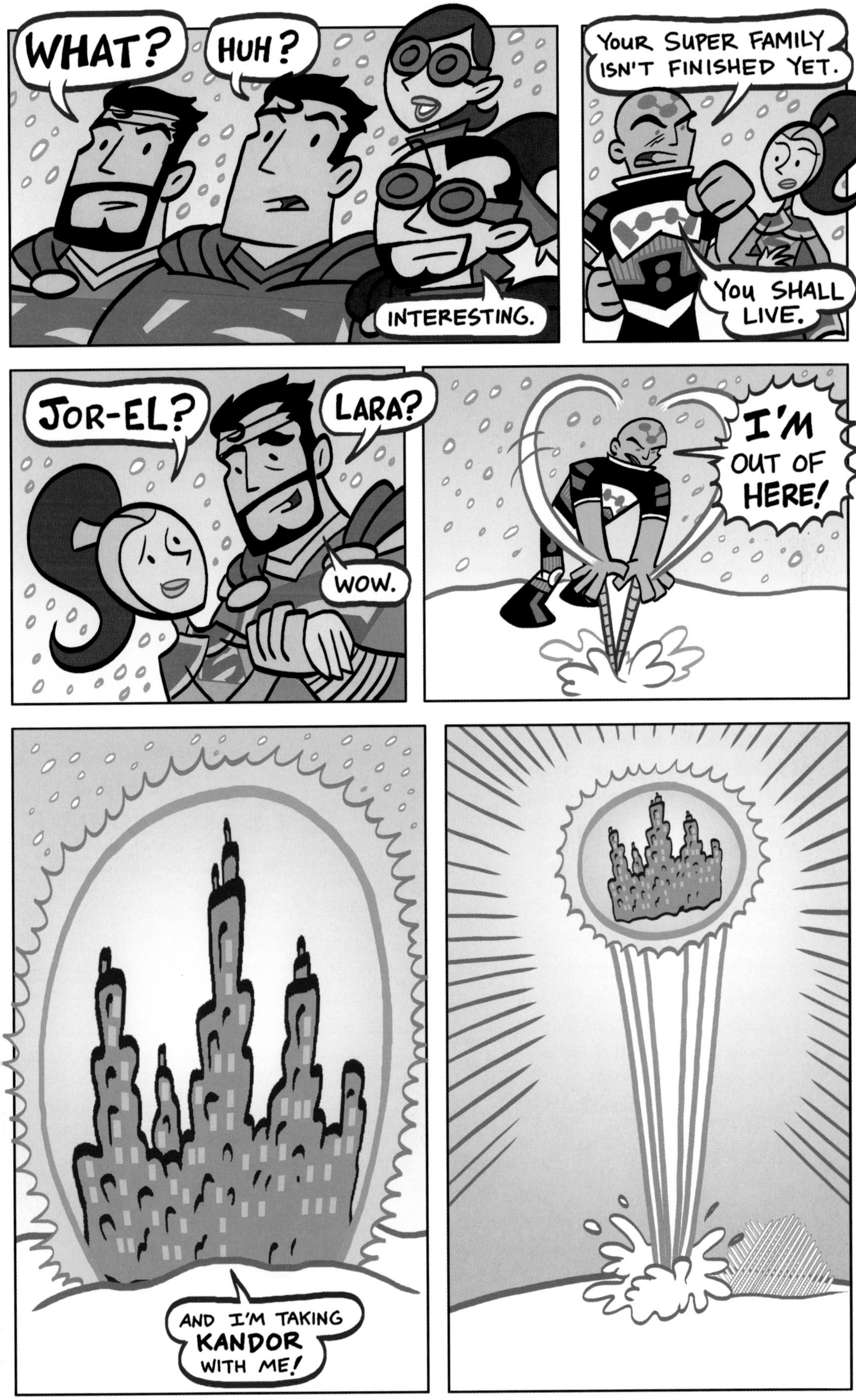
WHAT?
HUH?
INTERESTING.
YOUR SUPER FAMILY ISN'T FINISHED YET.
YOU SHALL LIVE.
JOR-EL?
LARA?
WOW.
I'M OUT OF HERE!
AND I'M TAKING KANDOR WITH ME!

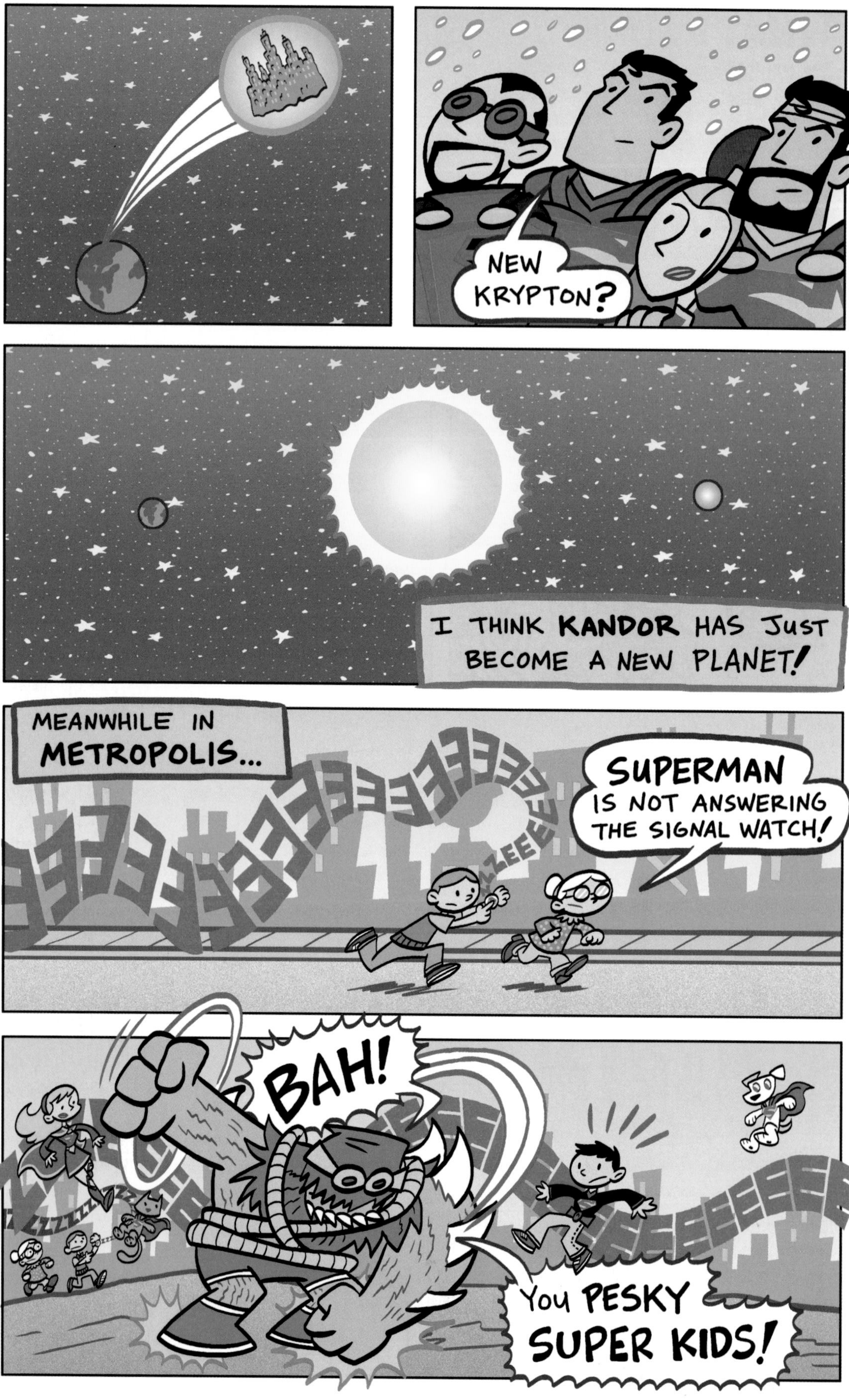
NEW KRYPTON?
I THINK KANDOR HAS JUST BECOME A NEW PLANET!
MEANWHILE IN METROPOLIS...
SUPERMAN IS NOT ANSWERING THE SIGNAL WATCH!
BAH!
You PESKY SUPER KIDS!

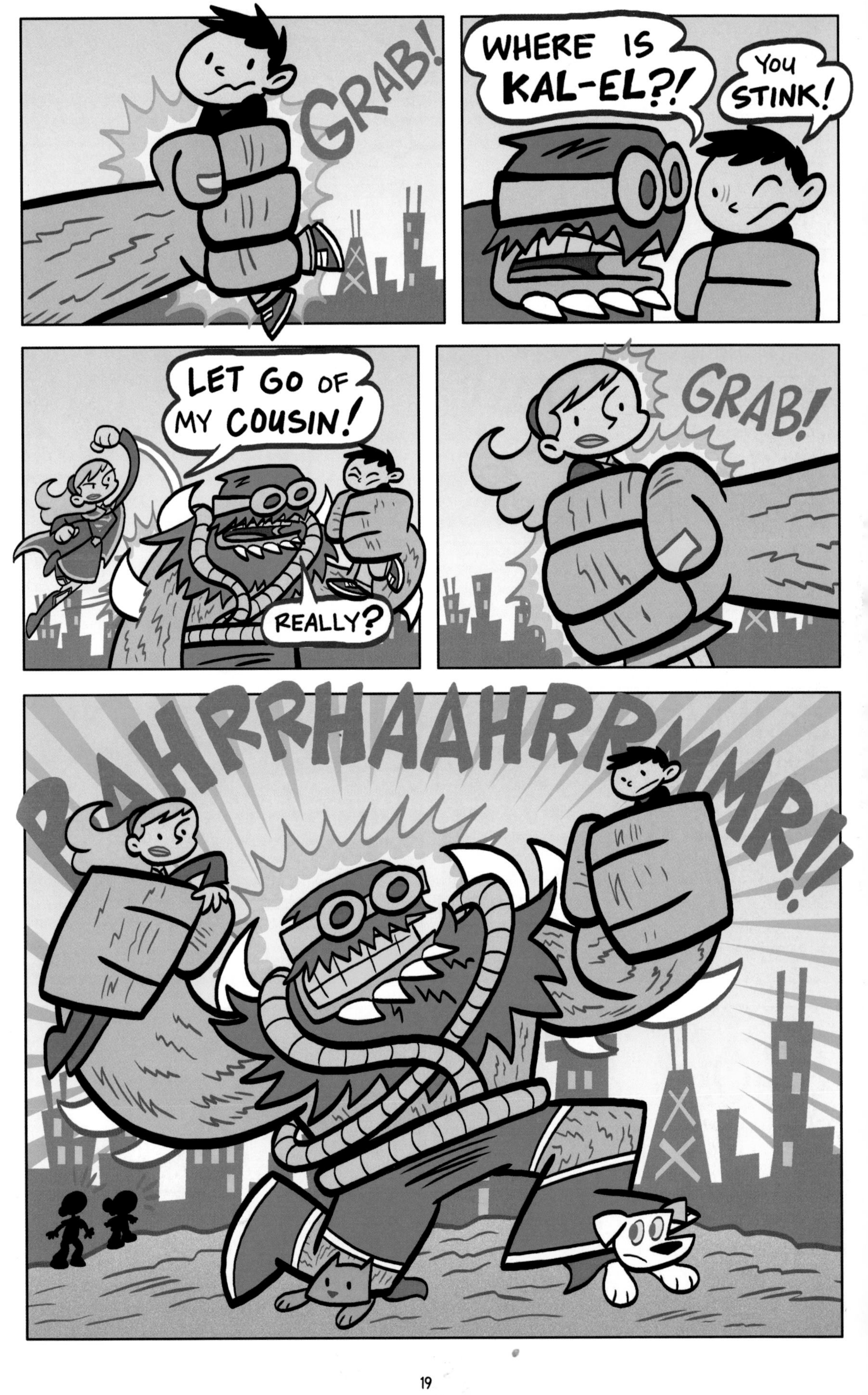
GRAB!
WHERE IS KAL-EL?!
YOU STINK!
LET GO OF MY COUSIN!
REALLY?
GRAB!
RAHRRHAAHRRMMR!!

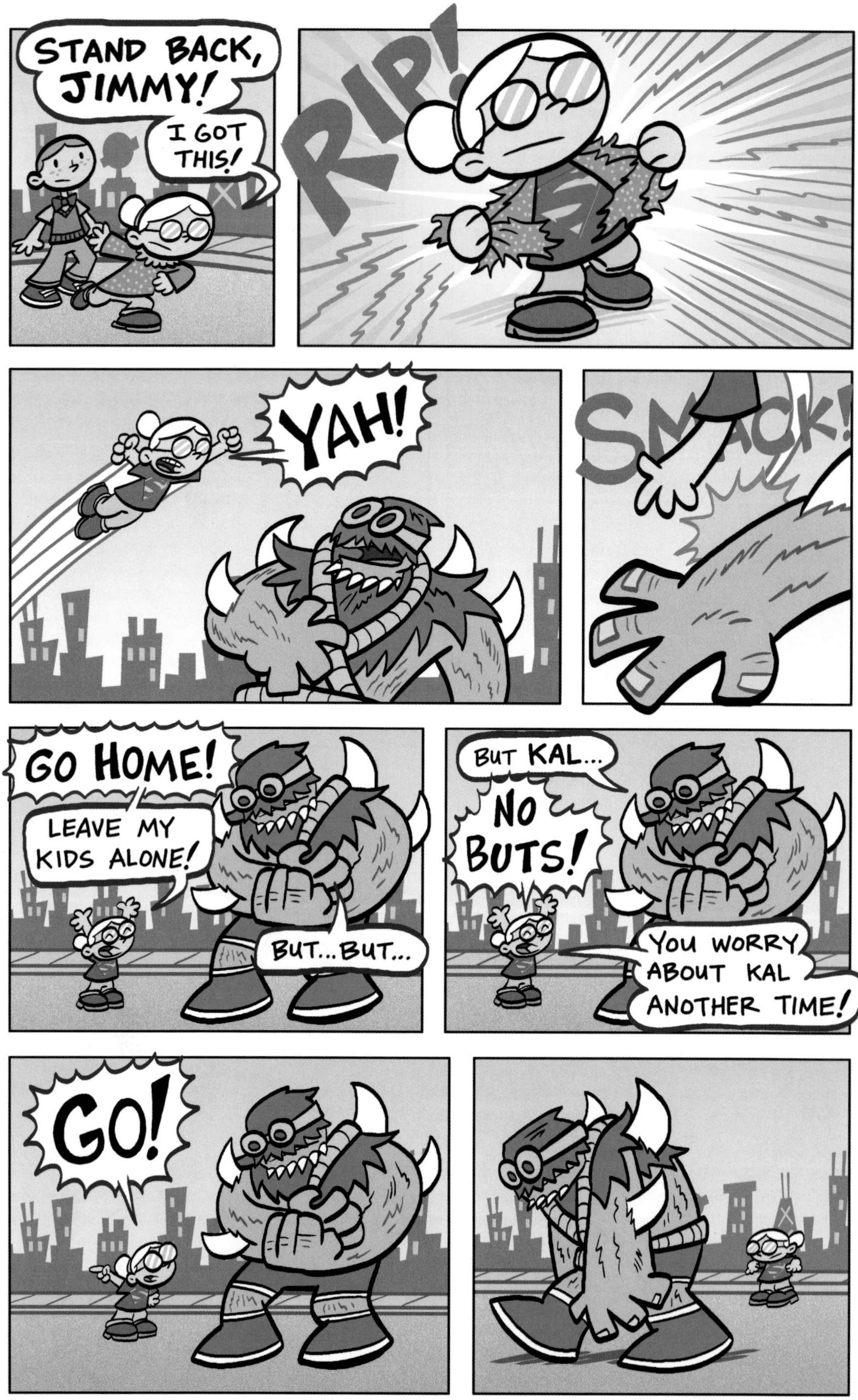
STAND BACK, JIMMY!
I GOT THIS!
RIP!
YAH!
SMACK!
GO HOME!
LEAVE MY KIDS ALONE!
BUT...BUT...
BUT KAL...
NO BUTS!
YOU WORRY ABOUT KAL ANOTHER TIME!
GO!

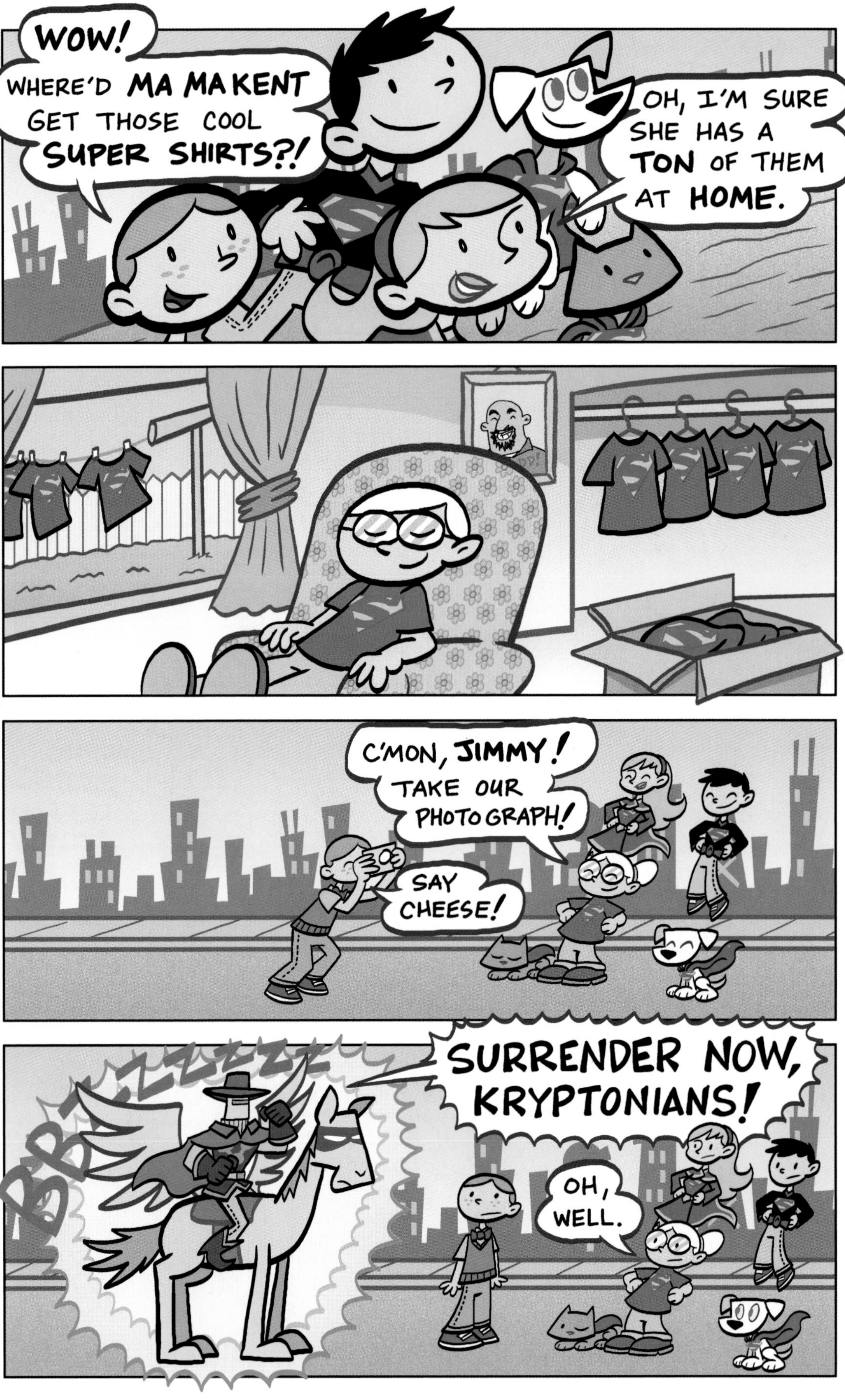
WOW!
WHERE'D MA MA KENT GET THOSE COOL SUPER SHIRTS?!
OH, I'M SURE SHE HAS A TON OF THEM AT HOME.
C'MON, JIMMY! TAKE OUR PHOTOGRAPH!
SAY CHEESE!
BRZZZZZZ
SURRENDER NOW, KRYPTONIANS!
OH, WELL.

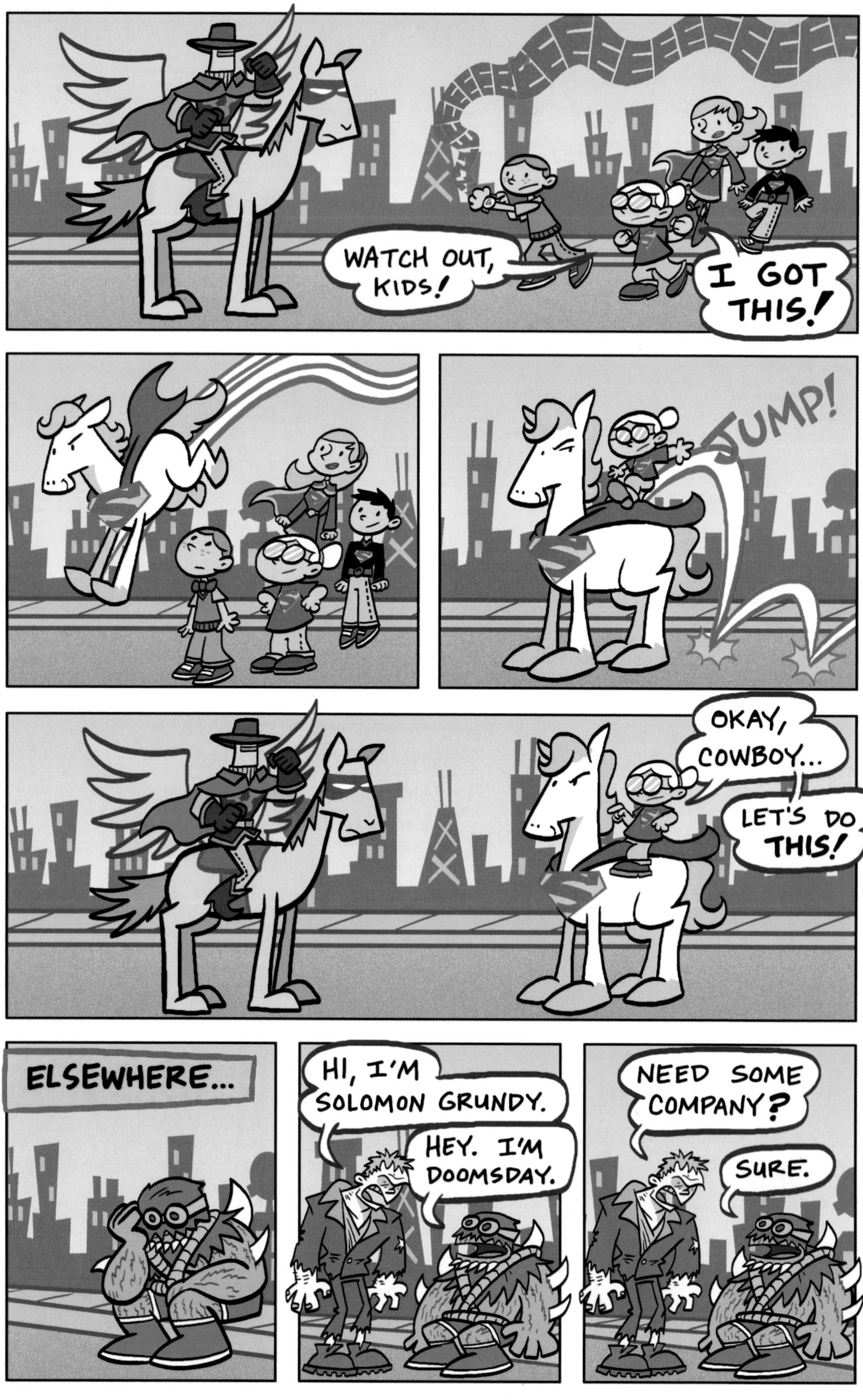

WATCH OUT, KIDS!
I GOT THIS!
JUMP!
OKAY, COWBOY...
LET'S DO THIS!
ELSEWHERE...
HI, I'M SOLOMON GRUNDY.
HEY. I'M DOOMSDAY.
NEED SOME COMPANY?
SURE.

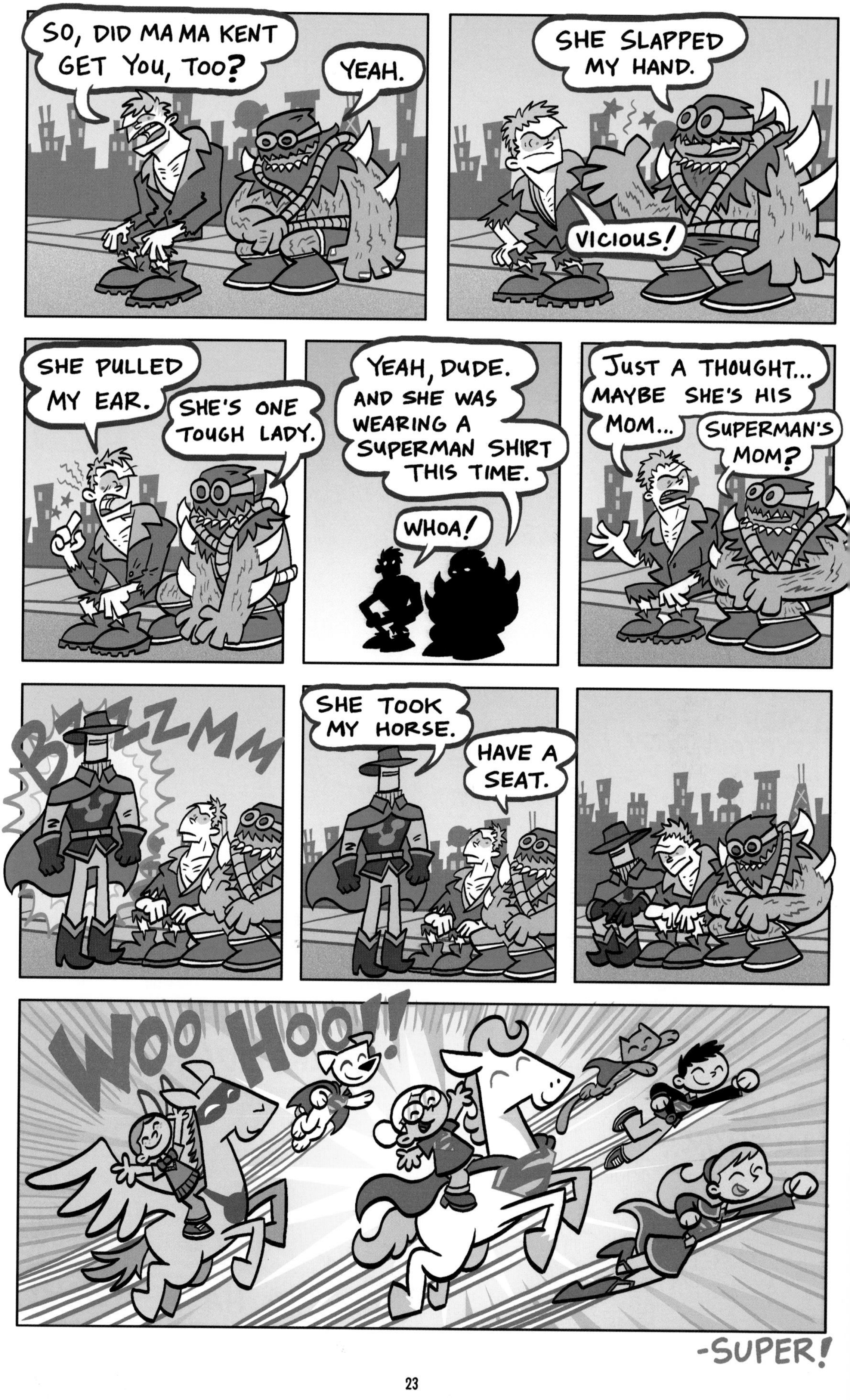
SO, DID MA MA KENT GET YOU, TOO?
YEAH.
SHE SLAPPED MY HAND.
VICIOUS!
SHE PULLED MY EAR.
SHE'S ONE TOUGH LADY.
YEAH, DUDE. AND SHE WAS WEARING A SUPERMAN SHIRT THIS TIME.
WHOA!
JUST A THOUGHT... MAYBE SHE'S HIS MOM...
SUPERMAN'S MOM?
BZZZMM
SHE TOOK MY HORSE.
HAVE A SEAT.
WOO HOO!!
-SUPER!

MEANWHILE, AT SIDEKICK CITY ELEMENTARY...

SIDEKICK CITY ELEMENTARY

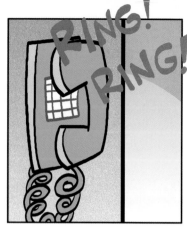

RING! RING!

LUNCH ROOM!

LUNCH LADY DARKSEID SPEAKING!

WHAT?

SPLAT!

MORE KRYPTONIANS?!

SPLAT!

A WHOLE PLANET OF THEM?

WHO IS THIS?!

IT IS I! LEX LUTHOR!!

BELIEVE IT TO BE TRUE, LORD DARKSEID!

THE PLAYING FIELD JUST GOT ALTERED!

HA HA HEE HOH!

—TO BE CONCLUDED!

SUPERMAN®
FAMILY ADVENTURES™

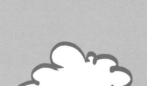

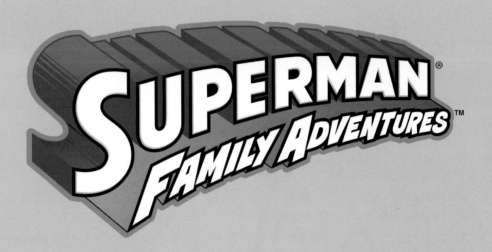

CREATORS

ART BALTAZAR IS A CARTOONIST MACHINE FROM THE HEART OF CHICAGO! HE DEFINES CARTOONS AND COMICS NOT ONLY AS AN ART STYLE, BUT AS A WAY OF LIFE. CURRENTLY, ART IS THE CREATIVE FORCE BEHIND THE NEW YORK TIMES BEST-SELLING, EISNER AWARD-WINNING, DC COMICS SERIES TINY TITANS, AND THE CO-WRITER FOR BILLY BATSON AND THE MAGIC OF SHAZAM! AND CO-CREATOR OF SUPERMAN FAMILY ADVENTURES. ART IS LIVING THE DREAM! HE DRAWS COMICS AND NEVER HAS TO LEAVE THE HOUSE. HE LIVES WITH HIS LOVELY WIFE, ROSE, BIG BOY SONNY, LITTLE BOY GORDON, AND LITTLE GIRL AUDREY. RIGHT ON!

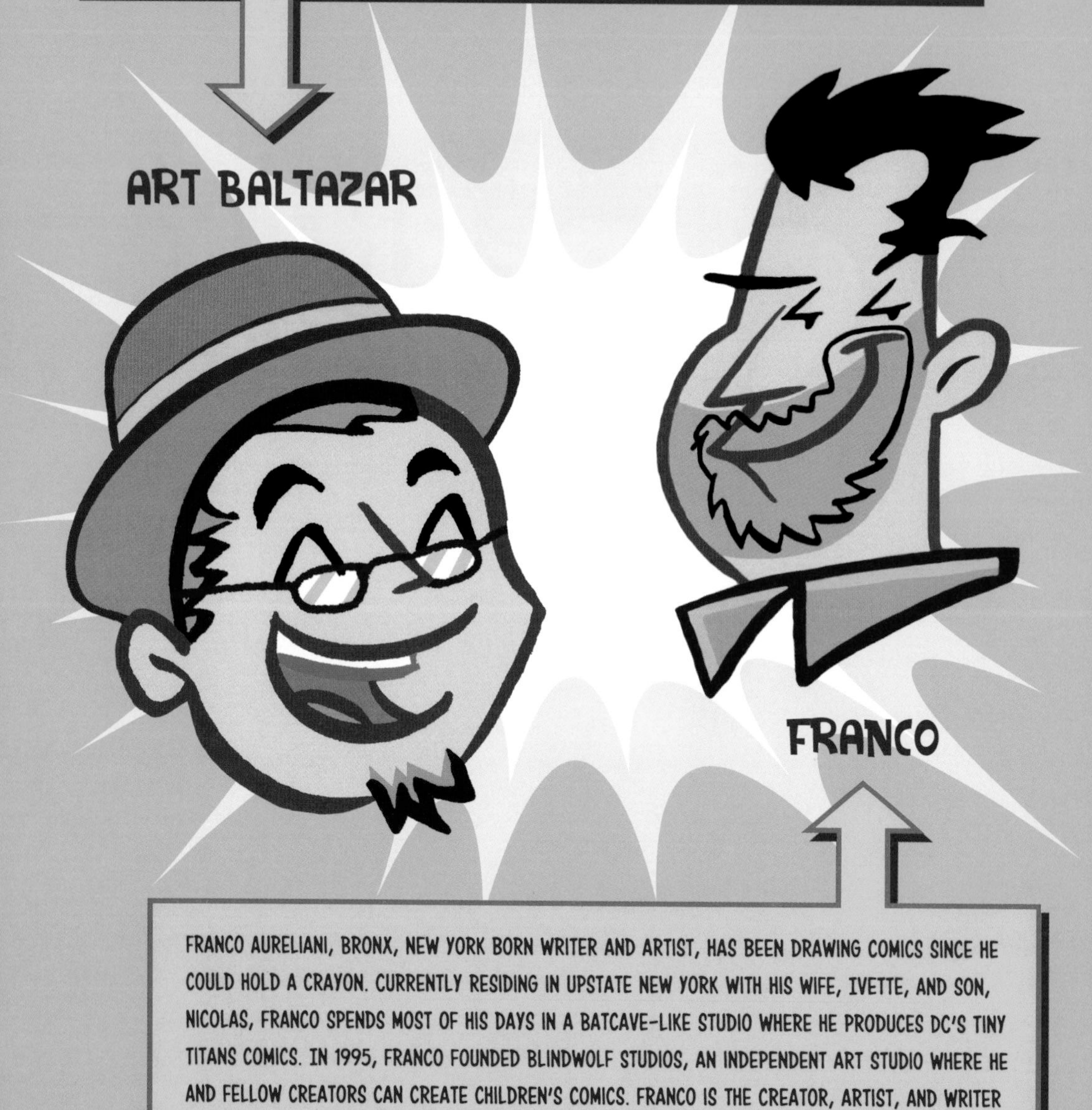
ART BALTAZAR
FRANCO

FRANCO AURELIANI, BRONX, NEW YORK BORN WRITER AND ARTIST, HAS BEEN DRAWING COMICS SINCE HE COULD HOLD A CRAYON. CURRENTLY RESIDING IN UPSTATE NEW YORK WITH HIS WIFE, IVETTE, AND SON, NICOLAS, FRANCO SPENDS MOST OF HIS DAYS IN A BATCAVE-LIKE STUDIO WHERE HE PRODUCES DC'S TINY TITANS COMICS. IN 1995, FRANCO FOUNDED BLINDWOLF STUDIOS, AN INDEPENDENT ART STUDIO WHERE HE AND FELLOW CREATORS CAN CREATE CHILDREN'S COMICS. FRANCO IS THE CREATOR, ARTIST, AND WRITER OF WEIRDSVILLE, L'IL CREEPS, AND EAGLE ALL STAR, AS WELL AS THE CO-CREATOR AND WRITER OF PATRICK THE WOLF BOY. WHEN HE'S NOT WRITING AND DRAWING, FRANCO ALSO TEACHES HIGH SCHOOL ART.

GLOSSARY

altered (AWL-turd)—changed into something

betrayal (bi-TRAY-uhl)—the act of breaking loyalty or trust with someone

collides (kuh-LIDEZ)—crashed together forcefully

demise (di-MIZE)—the end of something, or someone

doom (DOOM)—if you meet your doom, you suffer a terrible fate

enlarged (en-LARJD)—made bigger

glimpse (GLIMPS)—to see something briefly, or to sneak a peek at something

gruesome (GROO-suhm)—something that is gruesome is disgusting and horrible

rogue (ROHG)—if you go rogue, you separate yourself from the group and function on your own

surrender (suh-REN-dur)—to give up, or to admit that you are beaten in a fight or battle

VISUAL QUESTIONS & PROMPTS

1. THERE ARE MANY COLORS OF KRYPTONITE. WHAT DOES GREEN KRYPTONITE DO TO SUPERMAN? DO YOU KNOW WHAT ANY OTHER COLORS DO TO HIM?

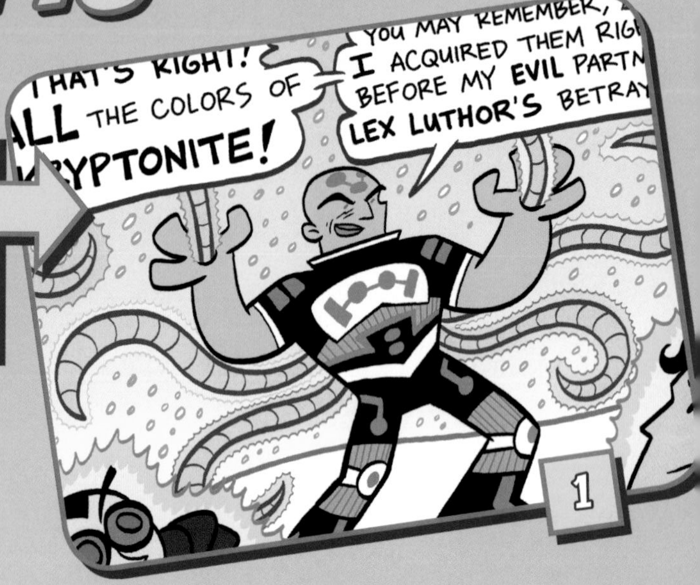

HAT'S RIGHT!
LL THE COLORS OF
YPTONITE!
YOU MAY REMEMBER,
I ACQUIRED THEM RIG
BEFORE MY EVIL PARTN
LEX LUTHOR'S BETRAY
1

2. WHAT DO THE GOLDEN LINES MEAN IN THE BACKGROUND? HOW DO THEY AFFECT THE WAY YOU SEE THE ILLUSTRATION?

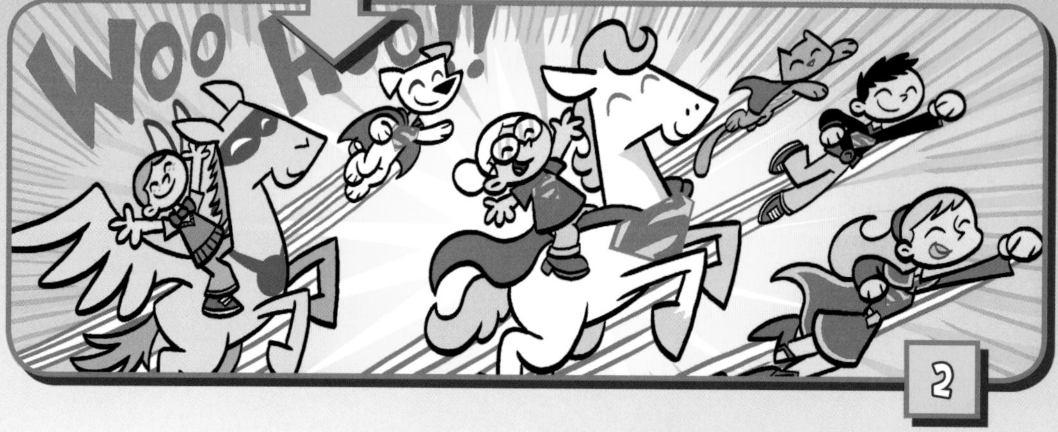

WOO
2

3. WHY DOES BRAINIAC SENSE TWO HEARTBEATS? READ THE REST OF THE PANELS ON PAGES 16-17 FOR CLUES.

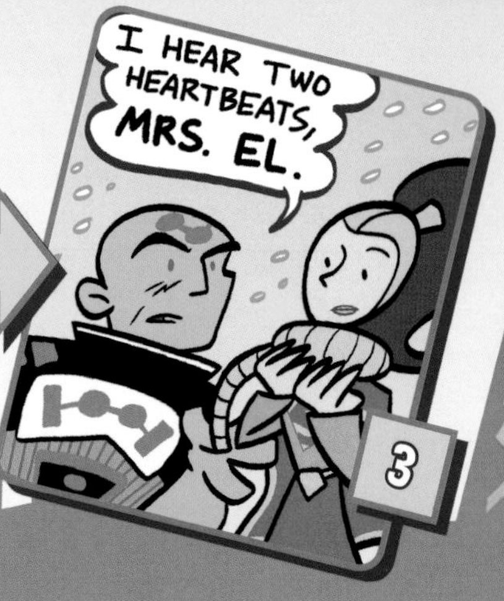

I HEAR TWO HEARTBEATS, MRS. EL.
3

4. WHAT WAS BRAINIAC GOING TO SAY IN THIS FIRST PANEL BEFORE HE STOPPED SPEAKING (INDICATED BY THE TWO HYPHENS AFTER "FA")?

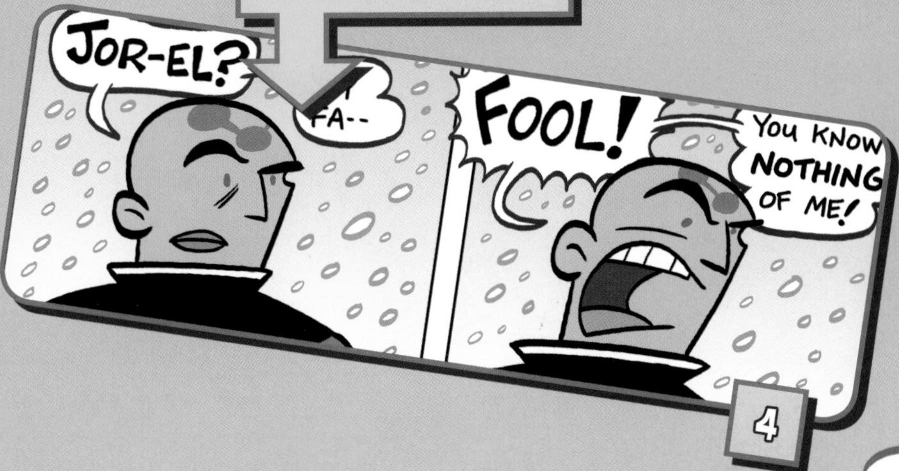
JOR-EL?
FA--
FOOL!
YOU KNOW NOTHING OF ME!
4

5. IN THESE PANELS, IDENTIFY AS MANY WAYS AS YOU CAN THAT MA KENT HINTS TO LOIS THAT HER SON, CLARK KENT, IS ACTUALLY SUPERMAN.

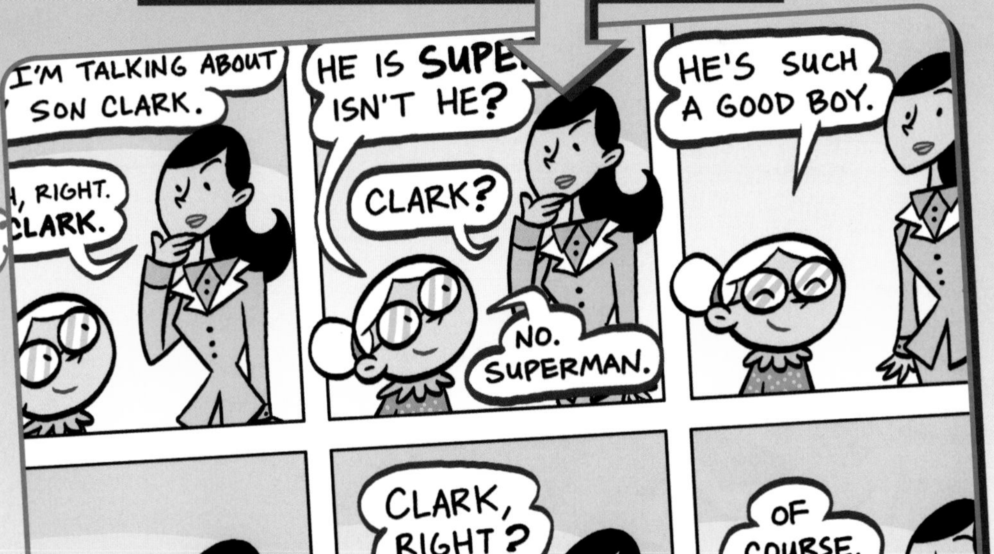
I'M TALKING ABOUT
SON CLARK.
RIGHT.
CLARK.
HE IS SUPE
ISN'T HE?
CLARK?
NO. SUPERMAN.
HE'S SUCH A GOOD BOY.
CLARK, RIGHT?
OF COURSE.
5

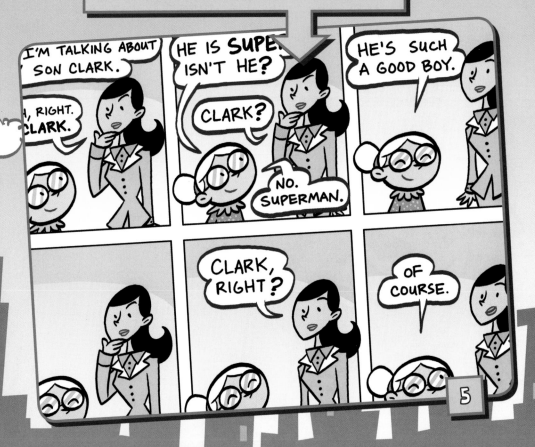

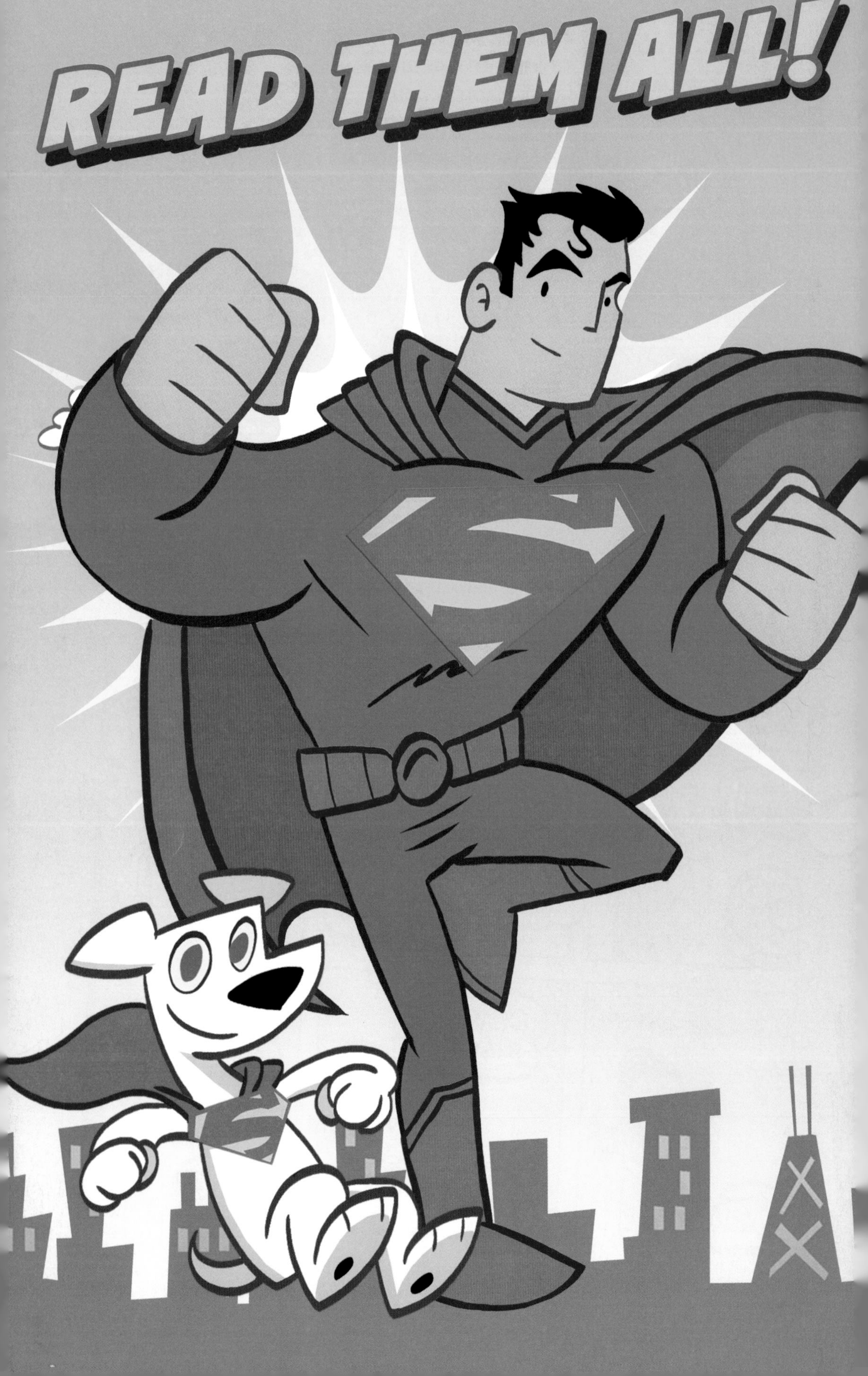
READ THEM ALL!

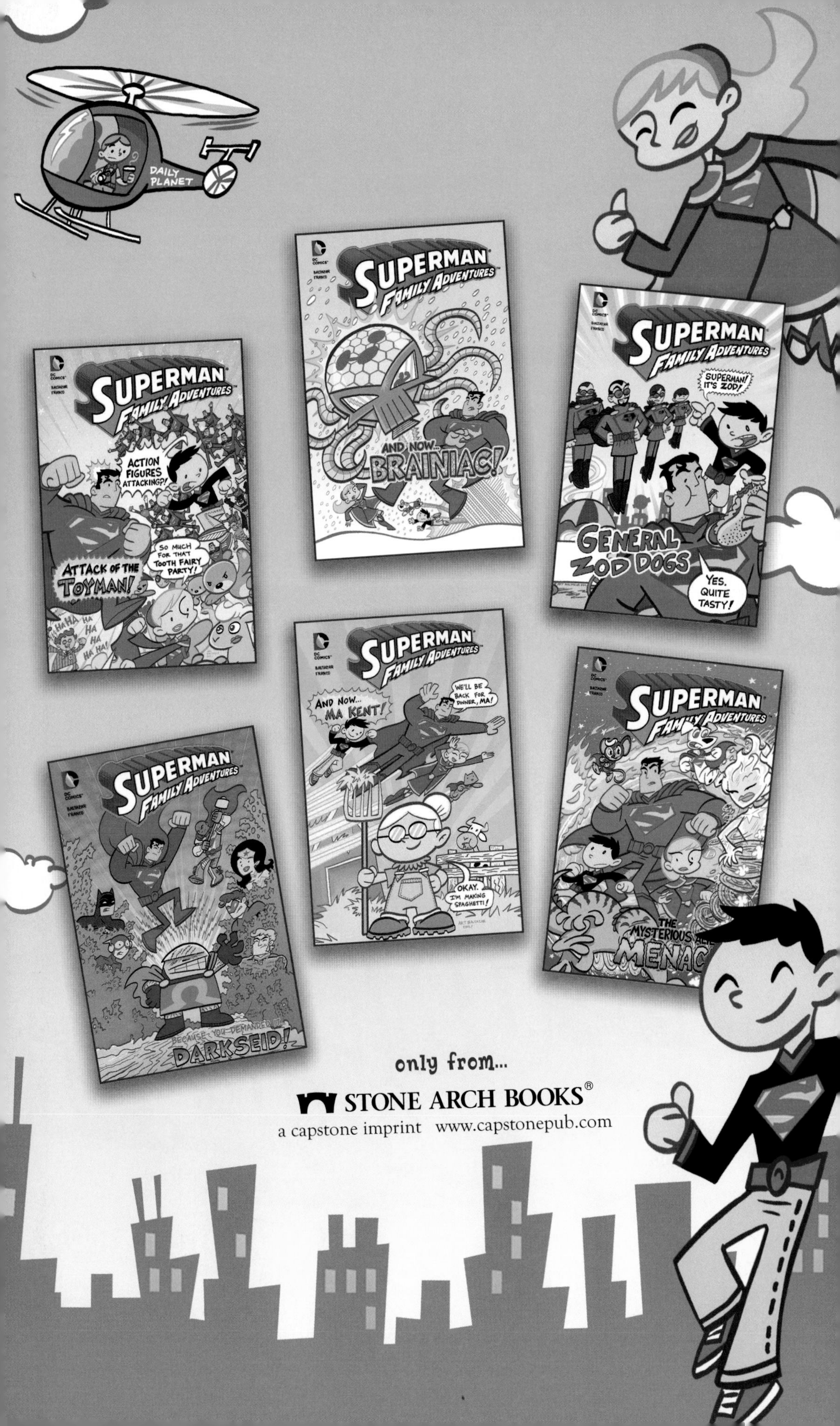
DAILY PLANET
SUPERMAN FAMILY ADVENTURES
ACTION FIGURES ATTACKING?!
SO MUCH FOR THAT TOOTH FAIRY PARTY!
ATTACK OF THE TOYMAN!
HA HA HA HA HA HA!
SUPERMAN FAMILY ADVENTURES
AND NOW... BRAINIAC!
SUPERMAN FAMILY ADVENTURES
SUPERMAN! IT'S ZOD!
GENERAL ZOD DOGS
YES. QUITE TASTY!
SUPERMAN FAMILY ADVENTURES
BECAUSE YOU DEMANDED IT
DARKSEID!
SUPERMAN FAMILY ADVENTURES
AND NOW... MA KENT!
WE'LL BE BACK FOR DINNER, MA!
OKAY. I'M MAKING SPAGHETTI!
SUPERMAN FAMILY ADVENTURES
THE MYSTERIOUS
only from...
STONE ARCH BOOKS®
a capstone imprint www.capstonepub.com

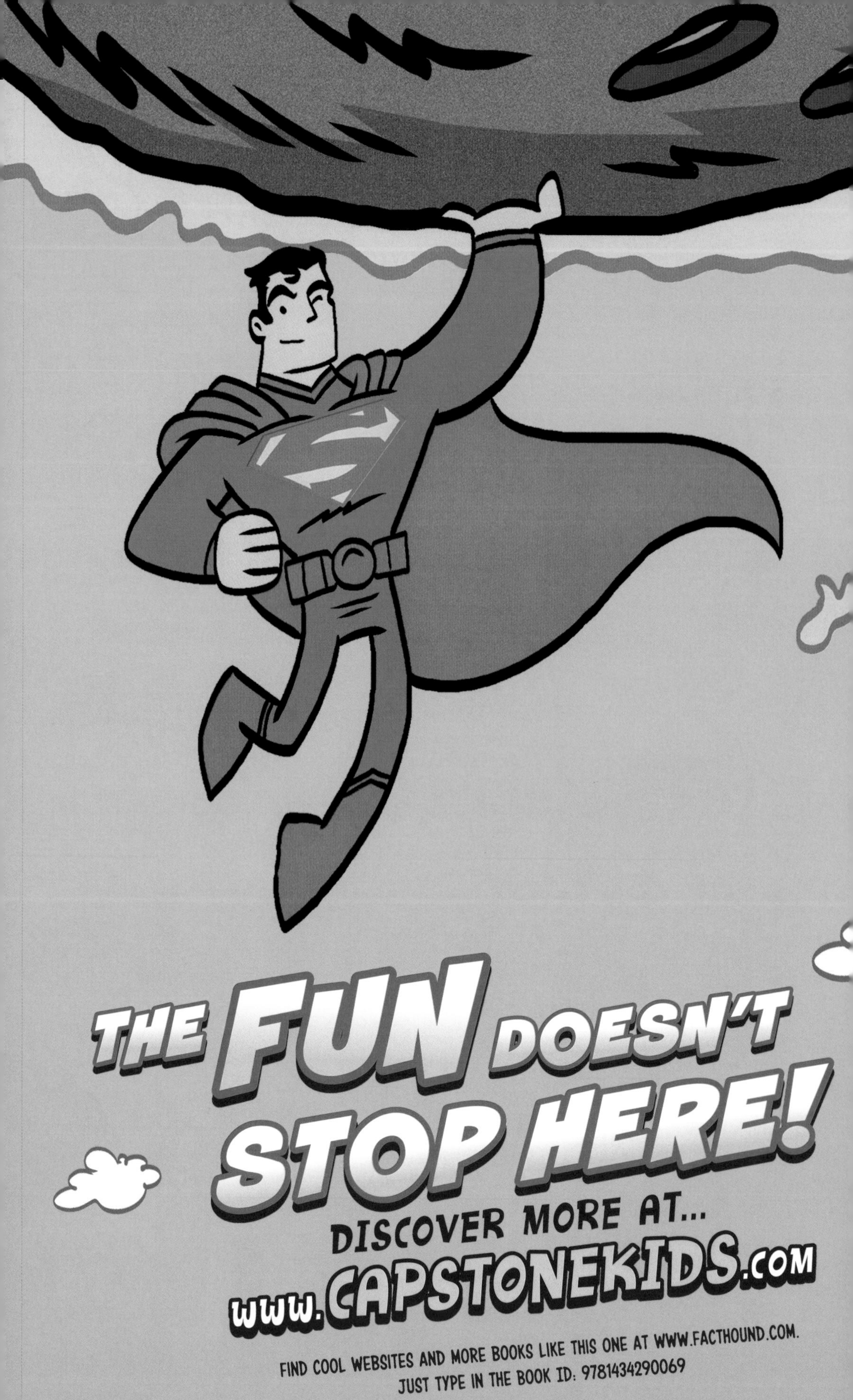